A CONVOCATION
of FIVE

PATRICK CONLEY

authorHOUSE®

AuthorHouse™
1663 Liberty Drive
Bloomington, IN 47403
www.authorhouse.com
Phone: 833-262-8899

Published by AuthorHouse 05/12/2021

ISBN: 978-1-6655-2560-2 (sc)
ISBN: 978-1-6655-2559-6 (e)

A FOREWORD & A FOREWARNING

All characters in this work are fictitious; accordingly, anyone looking for resemblances to living or deceased people will be disappointed. Fiction allows us an escape from reality and a retreat from the mundane even as it teases us, if only momentarily, into believing that this world of letters is real. However, if the characters and situations remain as flights of imagination, perhaps the story itself may depict some small element of truth.

STAGES

STAGE ONE

GROUSING AND PLANNING

"I JUST DON'T SEE WHY PHIL called this meeting. I mean, it's not as if we don't have more than enough meetings anyway. Besides, this disrupts my eating and sleeping patterns."

"Well, Pete, we wouldn't want to do that. I mean, with all that abundance of weighty substance hanging down from your sides, we all know how much you treasure eating and sleeping."

"Sly, you're always getting after me. You don't like these meetings any more than I do. They interrupt your byzantine intriguing or whatever it is you do. Besides, most of the time, you're nothing more than a common thief."

"Pete, you lack the finer sense. I'm not a thief. I'm simply rectifying the unjust distribution of wealth. I take from the rich and give to the poor. And I'm one of the poor."

"Sly, you're one of the lazy. You're too lazy to catch your own food."

"Look who's calling whom lazy. You spend most of the time just sleeping away, you slothful 'posssum."

"The proper term is opossum, my less than sophisticated friend. How would you like to be termed an 'accoon?"

Exasperated, Sly retorted. "No one ever says 'accoon, but just about anybody who is anybody uses the word,'possum. Remember that little ditty, 'O, say can you see the 'possum in the tree.'"

Carrie looked on at these two feuding companions with dark, indifferent eyes. "Those two are always bickering and whining," she reflected. "It's all so petty, and in the end, especially in our present condition, none of this fussing makes any difference. Those two will quit their infernal feuding once Phil lumbers in. Then they'll be all smiles and pretend to be the best of buddies. But Phil knows."

As if taking Carrie's thoughts as a cue, Phil did, indeed, noiselessly enter the convocation room. It really wasn't a room, for it was open to the sky and consisted merely of ropes designating the convocation area. But even in this open arena, Phil loomed large. It wasn't just his size that was imposing although he was huge. Phil could enter any space and soon be acknowledged as king. He looked like a philosopher deep in thought, but he could also lull one into complacency and then play a trick. His favorite ruse was to appear so engrossed in thought that others would approach him slowly, fascinated by his eyes that seemed to stare into a world of profound mysteries. Then he'd splash the onlookers with water from the reflective pool that lay nearby him. His 776 pound weight lent authority to that splash, making it a tidal wave. Then he'd slowly make his way some distance and set his trap for his next victim. But it was all a game and no one was ever hurt. In his other life, Phil was renowned as king of the zoo. Now in his next life, he presided over a small convocation of other creatures who had passed on from terrestrial concerns—or had they?

"I have assembled all of you together to begin the work on a special assignment." Phil intoned.

"Does this mean we're going to have lots of meetings?" Pete interrupted.

"Yes, Pete, we've enjoyed a bit of a vacation lately, but now we've been given a new assignment."

"Who gave us this assignment? I want to go back to sleep." Pete objected strenuously, even managing to scurry around in a frenzied rage.

"Pete, only you could ask such a question. That car must have smashed your brains out when it squished you." Sly uttered his high-pitched snicker and started washing his hands in the air as no water lay nearby.

Pete countered with his own snide retort. "Well, Sly, at least I didn't get myself treed and then shot down. My demise was strictly accidental while yours resulted from your own negligence and arrogance."

At this comment, Carrie took flight and flapped her enormous wings until she could soar and just catch the wind. She looked down on all of them from on high before she swooped down to take her place at the convocation. Her flight served as a silent remonstrance to Sly and Pete's constant bickering.

Phil looked on, rubbing his chin, and fully aware that all of this foolishness would die down—at least for a little while—once they settled into the business of reviewing the facts of the case in question and developing a preliminary evaluation to be forwarded upstairs. However, one immediate and rather pressing matter remained. Phil had to introduce a new member to the rest of their convocation—one that Sly might find particularly difficult to accept. Phil determined to use the squabbling of Pete and Sly to his advantage. He'd first make them feel a bit guilty for their self-centered squabbling. He shot them a look that froze their mouths and caused them to settle down. They both knew how futile it was to upset Phil.

"Our first order of business is to greet a new member of our convocation. Let me introduce to you Amanda."

Sly checked a sinister hiss before it left his mouth. Pete started to complain, "We don't need anyone else. We work fine together."

"Is that a fact?" Phil replied in a deadpan voice. Then he stood up to his full length and began his chest thumping, which proclaimed that it was time to settle down to business. "It's time to do our present job and leave the past life behind you. We have work to do. And the addition of Amanda to our little team is long overdue. Pete, you provide insight into matters of the flesh. Sly, you know how to navigate devious mental matters. You can solve problems with practical expertise. Carrie reminds us of the broader perspective. There's just one insight lacking."

"Oh, and what's that?" Sly asked trying hard not sound facetious even though he was.

"Emotion. Amanda has the gift of being attuned to nuances of emotion. Just now, Sly, she sensed your snide innuendo no matter how hard you tried to disguise it."

Just then Carrie flapped her wings and stretched out her bald neck, red in a gruesome sort of way.

"Enough," Pete cried. "Carrie reminds me of something I'd rather forget. Let's get down to business. Oh, and welcome, Amanda. We don't really hate each other that much. It's just hard to deal with an assembly of different species."

Reluctantly, Sly agreed and added in a somewhat sincere tone, "Welcome, Amanda, to our little team. And, for once, Pete is right. It's past time to get down to business."

"I hope that all of you realize that you have prolonged the meeting—a meeting you say you don't like—by another ten minutes or so." Phil spoke indifferently in a monotone as if he were just making a casual observation and not chastising anyone, but they all knew that their own behavior was to blame.

Nevertheless, whatever contrite thoughts that raced through their minds soon faded away. Phil resumed his outlining of their task. "I've read over Thomas Albright's dossier thoroughly and noticed a few constant themes." Here Phil surveyed the eyes of his four colleagues. Amanda, the newest member, stood attentively, her deep pool of eyes fixed squarely on Phil's. Pete's eyelids were half closed, while Carrie maintained her characteristic look of indifference. Sly's eyes darted from side to side as if he were looking for an angle. "Sly, you seem to be questioning something. What concerns you?"

"What if you've overlooked a theme or two, then what? I mean, you're fallible, just like the rest of us."

"Well, Sly, you're welcome to study the entire dossier. Here it is in three volumes."

Resentful over having his bluff called, Sly asked, "Why are there only three copies of the dossier when there's five of us to read it."

"Actually, Sly, there's only one copy of the dossier. It's in three volumes, with each volume running over 80,000 words. You are welcome to read the entire three volumes at your leisure."

Sly mumbled almost under his breath, "That's all right as long as the dossier is always available for reference."

"All right, then, here are some of the themes I've noticed. You may see more. The dossier will be available whenever you wish to consult it. I'm placing it here." Sly darted his eyes over to the place and then even more quickly steered his vision towards Phil's eyes. "The first three themes we'll discuss will be the following: 1) Respect for Animals; 2) Ambivalence Towards War; 3) Respect for Education."

"Well, Phil, those three don't have much in common, now do they?" Sly interjected.

"Yeah, what about respect for eating and sleeping? If we're taking a chronological approach, those respects would come first." Pete chimed in.

Carrie looked on with indifference; however, she was intrigued by the theme related to war. "Didn't the Saxons describe a battlefield as a crow's feast?" Carrie observed silently.

Amanda broke her silence. "Phil, if you concur, I'd like to discuss that first theme, Respect for Animals. I think it's one we could all agree on."

"Thanks, Amanda, actually, that theme or through-line in Tom's life was the reason his life-dossier was assigned to our small convocation in the first place. Our boss knew I had known Tom in our previous lives, so he assigned me the case."

"Look, if the decision to approve this Albright guy for admission has already been made, then why are we wasting our time with this ad hoc convocation? This is just another example of bureaucratic redundancy and meeting for meeting's sake." Sly stamped down his right forepaw for emphasis.

Phil stroked his chin before replying, but Amanda responded quickly. "I've seen many a nice boy turn into a vicious adult. We should regard this as a starting point, not an end point."

"Eager to get this first session over with so he could go back to sleep, Pete agreed. "Yeah, let's hear it out. Two of us here, maybe all five of us have experienced humans' cruelty and indifference towards animals, so let's listen. I suggest we spend no more than ten minutes discussing this issue before we move on. In fact, I think we ought to devote a maximum of ten minutes to each theme or through line or whatever you want to call it. That way, we'll know when to stop and not just go on and on and on."

"Is that a formal motion, Pete?" Phil asked.

"Yes, Phil, it is."

"I second the motion." Amanda added, hoping to find some consensus.

"Any discussion?" Phil looked around. Not even Sly wanted to voice any objections. "Are we all agreed?" Phil looked around, and saw three paws and one wing raised in assent. "All right, we have a consensus. This first session will end in thirty minutes or less. Unless someone else would like to volunteer for the office, I believe that Carrie would be the best choice for timekeeper."

"Carrie's always aware of time, especially end-time," Sly agreed.

"Then we're set. Let me provide a summary of Tom Albright's first encounter with animals, especially me. It was back in the summer of 1954. Back in those days, zoos didn't think much of the animals' welfare. Zookeepers did, but the ones who controlled the purse strings had a kind of tunnel vision. They thought that the only purpose of the zoo was entertainment for humans, well, that and some education, too. Back then I was called the King of the Zoo because I provided a lot of the entertainment. Well, anyway, I was locked up in a concrete grey cage with a pool of water just so I could cool off. You know those hot, humid days in the tropics seemed mild in contrast to those Midwestern summers. Well, anyway, three boys around ten years old were standing outside my cage, trying to provoke me, You know they called me stuff like 'Banana Boy' and 'Dumb Monkey'—even though I'm not a monkey, just a relative of that species. Then they started jumping up and down and scratching their sides and making what they thought were gorilla sounds. Well, Tom and his parents walked by. I could tell by his eyes that Tom's dad looked disgusted not by me but by his fellow humans. Tom tugged at his father's arm and whispered, 'Why are they so mean, Daddy. Maybe they should be the ones locked up.' His dad responded something about how the boys were probably just aping their parents. I sortta like that, 'aping their parents.' So I just knuckled my way over to the pond real slowly so as not to arouse any suspicion and stroked my chin for a few seconds. Then I splashed those three boys and, man, did I ever give them a soaking. It wasn't any kind splash either. It was one that almost knocked them off their feet. Then I coolly made my way over to the backside of the fake tree in my cage and looked as if nothing had happened.

"Later, long after I had passed on to the new life, I learned from the big cats—you know the lions, panthers, and tigers and pumas—that Tom Albright also empathized with their plight. They, too, were locked up in concrete and steel cages so that all they could do was pace back and forth and endure the mockery of humans. Things did change, though, for the better. And for this, I'll have to give humans some credit. Now the Great Apes and the Great Cats enjoy far more spacious and natural setting even though doing so cost lots of money and sometimes made it hard for people to see. You still get a few idiot humans who think of the zoo as a freak show, but not near as many as they were back then. In his own small way, people like Tom made that change happen. So, any way, that's my first encounter with Tom Albright."

"That's only one encounter, Phil. Did you have others or was this a one hit wonder?" Sly asked sarcastically.

"A good question, Sly. No, Tom was a regular visitor to the zoo, partially because there was no admission fee and his parents didn't have much money but more because he liked seeing me, especially when I seemed to be at peace. He always looked at me so sympathetically."

Amanda added, "This is a good start. I'm getting to like this Albright guy already."

"Are we going to spend this much time going over every mushy detail of Tom and the animals?" Pete whined. Aren't the ten minutes about up?"

"No," Carrie replied. "In fact you've got eight minutes left if you want to use all of the allotted time."

"Please, not eight more minutes of this!" Sly moaned. "Okay, we get it. The kid was sympathetic, but the real issue remains, what was his attitude like in later years—when he was an adult and could make his own decisions. Even Amanda realizes that not all sweet kids grow up to be sweet adults."

"This is just the first installment, Sly. There will be others." Phil said definitively.

"So how many more meetings will this take?" Pete whined, knowing full well that he had asked a rhetorical question.

"We'll survey his life from five or perhaps a few more perspectives," Phil stated.

"So how old is this guy as he approaches death?" Pete inquired, secretly hoping that this Tom fellow would pass on as a young man.

"He's in his late seventies, Pete."

"So, this is going to take a while, right?"

"Yes, Pete, that's why we're digesting all this in small bits. We now have less than twenty minutes to discuss two other themes in his early youth."

"Well, I like the boy already," Amanda added. "Let's hear more."

Sly had determined to ride out the next twenty minutes with no more interruptions. He figured that Phil would just add on more time to the thirty minute session if he tried to take it off task.

"This next theme concerns ambivalence towards war." Phil paused to see if the others were paying attention. Carrie flapped her wings at the mention of war, for battles meant carrion and a plentiful supply of rotting meat.

"Like most boys of his age, Tom's father had served in World War II. In a bureaucratic twist of fate, he had enlisted in the Army because he was dreadfully afraid of water because he couldn't swim. Once in the army, he was assigned to amphibious tanks, so he had the dubious distinction of participating in amphibious assaults for three years. Young Tom knew this, but his father seldom spoke of his army days. One day, though, when his father was working, Tom sneaked in to peek at his father's desk drawer. There he found a bronze star for bravery. He also found an armband with a sergeant's three stripes. Tom couldn't contain his joy. 'My Dad's a hero. He never told me about it. Wait till I tell the other guys.' Tom went off to find his friends, but none were home. Then he thought about it. 'My Dad's got to have some reason for not saying anything. I wonder what it is.' Later that same day, when his father had come home to relax, Tom turned on the TV to a channel that was televising a World War II movie, *The Sands of Iwo Jima*. In the early fifties, these films garnered large audiences. Tom's father started reading a newspaper as he sat in his chair. "Dad, how come you never watch war movies?" Tom asked. He saw his father get up and walk towards the kitchen as he simply said, 'Tom, I don't watch them because they're not true. That's not how it happened.' His father had spoken definitively. There was no questioning to be had. That was it. Tom was tied in a knot. One end pulled him towards his father's loathing of war; the other towards Hollywood's glorification of it."

Tom's father nailed it, " Carrie cried out, breaking her habitual reticence. "The guy was right. I've seen lots of guys crying out for their mothers as they tried to tuck in their innards that seeped out through open wounds. They never went peacefully, with their heads resting in the hands of a comrade as they whispered 'Give my ma (or sometimes fiancée or wife) this letter, would ya.' Then in the movie script, their head eased off to the side and their eyes closed. Most corpses have eyes pried wide open. I should know. That's what we carrion feeders gulp down first. Not much glory in that."

"Carrie, thanks for the insight." Phil wanted to change the topic. "Then there's more. Tom never thought to bring up the matter to his Dad again. Somehow, even as a young boy, Tom sensed that the topic would remain almost taboo. A few weeks later, he learned why. After dinner one night, his father had gone back to his bedroom and started walking in ever smaller circles. Then he fell as Tom's mother screamed. Quickly collecting herself, though, she opened a desk drawer and pulled out a tongue depressor as if she had done dozen of times before. Tom hadn't known it, but she had gone through the agony of this episode over and over again. She opened Dad's mouth and kept him from swallowing his tongue. All the while Tom looked on in horror. After a hellish eternity of waiting, Tom witnessed his mother easing his Dad into bed, where he would sleep peacefully.

"'Mom, what happened? Will Dad be all right? Why did this happen?' Tom's questions rushed out in a frenzied torrent.

"'Tom, your father just had an epileptic seizure. I had to keep him from swallowing his tongue and suffocating. It was the war. His tank got blown up. He spent months in the hospital. That's why he has to take so many pills.'

"'But the pills don't always work, do they, Mom.'

"'Not always. Come on, Tom, let's go in the kitchen and let your Dad rest. He should be fine in the morning.'"

"Tom had other experiences with war, but only vicarious ones as a boy. Still, his mind couldn't resolve the tension between what he had seen and heard his father say and what the films on TV brought into the living room."

"Is that it for the second theme, Phil?" Pete asked. "I don't like hearing about this sort of stuff."

"None of us do," Amanda added.

"Sometimes the truth is hard to digest," added Carrie.

Sly kept his thoughts to himself. He wondered why Tom's Dad couldn't sit around drinking beer and bragging about his war stories the way some guys did. Finally, though, he couldn't hold his thoughts in any longer. "Hell, maybe the guy couldda capitalized on his exploits and gone into politics and made a name for himself."

"Maybe you're right, Sly. Humans are just like a lot of dogs—always fighting over who is the leader of the pack," Amanda noted.

"Do their leaders get to eat more than the ones they lord it over?' Pete asked.

"Yeah, I know that for a fact. In my days of rummaging through trashcans, I observed that there's quite a different stench coming from the cans of the rich than from the poor. Of course, it all stinks the same in the end. Still, there's something to be said for the putrid aroma of decaying T-bone steak."

"Thanks for the observation, Sly. It is duly noted," Phil replied, struggling to keep his distaste in check. "No, Tom's father did what a lot of other guys returning from the Big War did. He went to school on the G.I. Bill and worked part-time. Of course, that meant that he had to stay close to home. Besides, he also did what a lot of other veterans did back in those days."

"Yeah, what's that?" Sly interjected with snide overtones. "Did he get hooked up in some get-rich-quick scam and then go busted?"

"No, Sly, he didn't. There was a brief moment when someone approached him with a scheme to get rich off uranium. The atomic bomb changed people's perspectives quite a bit. No, Sly, he did what countless other vets did: he got married. Those guys just wanted to settle down and forget about the barbarity of war. Sometimes they weren't even sure who their enemy was. Later, Tom learned from reading one of his father's letters home that on one island invasion a huge firefight lit up the night skies as rockets, grenades, and artillery blasts deafened the heavens and blotted out the stars. Machine gun fire tore through branches and put everyone on frayed nerves. Then the tanks began rolling and rolling over everything in their way, including the tents of the American soldiers."

"A big counterattack by the Japanese, huh," Sly added.

"No, no Japanese guns were fired. The men had gone berserk. Apparently from what Tom read, one shell-shocked sergeant started it all when he began firing into the jungle because he thought he had heard a noise. Then others joined in, and then they all went crazy. One guy had his leg broken when a tree that a tank had uprooted toppled on his leg. Another guy suffered lacerations from flying debris. Other than that there were only frayed nerves and that vague, empty gut sensation that comes when you feel you've done nothing other than to make an ass of yourself. Tom's dad found his tent collapsed, as he had to run a zigzag pattern to avoid the tanks that were careening about. It was just chaos. After the war, the vets just wanted to flee from that chaos. They wanted to get married, settle down and raise a family that would never experience the ravages of war. They also did one other thing: they went to school to learn if there was any sense in the world at all. Most of the combat vets had come from working class families, so they also knew that the overwhelming majority of those who suffered and died during war were the poor and uneducated."

"So, tell me again about that uranium mining scheme. Did it pay off?" Sly inquired eagerly.

"I'm not sure you listened to what I said after I mentioned the scheme that amounted to nothing more than a fleeting temptation," Phil lectured. "Although Tom's father did involve himself with radium, he never went mining."

"So, did he get hooked up in black market schemes to deal in uranium? "Sly asked.

"Yeah, did he get rich quick and then live off the fat of the land?" Pete asked.

"I'm sorry to disappoint the two of you, but Tom's dad worked part-time in the radiation labs while he went to college. In those days, no one knew that much about radiation, so the lab technicians handled the isotopes with their bare hands."

"Did that hurt them?" Amanda wanted to know.

"Not outwardly, inwardly I'm not sure. Sometimes it takes years and years before the effects surface."

"That's true," Carrie added. "Some of my colleagues from Japan reported on the corpses of those who died years after the Hiroshima and Nagasaki blasts. They had a funny odor, acrid and unpalatable."

"Well, I'll eat just about anything that doesn't move," Pete proclaimed.

"To get back on target," Phil stated objectively, "if we're going to finish this session on time we'll have to start winding matters up. How much time is left, Ms. Timekeeper?"

"Just a few minutes," Carrie responded prosaically. She had tired of all this talk and wanted to go back to soaring in the wind.

"That's what I thought," Phil replied with just a faint hint of sarcasm. In any event, Tom's father was resolved that his children would have the finest education they could. When Tom was born, his father rushed out and spent whatever money he could spare on children's book. When he wasn't reading from his college textbooks, Tom's father read to his infant son even when he had just turned one week old. His mother read to him, too, for she wanted her children to have the education she never did. Tom's own mother had never completed high school but valued books and reading more than most who just take education as a right. So, when money was tight—and it almost always was—she supplied the funds for whatever books were wanted. Tom's own grandfather also had never finished grade school, starting work at twelve. Tom remembered that his grandfather spent most of his free time puffing on his pipe and sitting in a battered but comfortable chair, his body too worn down by the strains of work. This, too, was a reason Tom's father valued education above all else. He used to say, 'They can take your house, your money, and sometimes your life, but they can't take your education away.'"

"So, now it's time to end this session, right, Carrie?" Pete asked yearning to rest his weary ears and go back to sleep.

Not even bothering to look at her watch, Carrie responded, "Yup, time's up."

STAGE TWO

DREAMS OF GLORY

P HIL CALLED FOR ANOTHER SESSION a week later. As usual, Pete mumbled away his futile protests. "I don't see why I have to get up, abandon my beloved treetop vista, and go to yet one more of these meetings. I thought that the big benefit of the second life would be NO MORE MEETINGS. Well, I was wrong. I guess I'll scurry on over to the Convocation Area and try to find a nice corner to hide in. Oh, no, there are no corners. Phil arranged the ropes in the round. Still, maybe I can get a choice spot the farthest way from the center of the circle. Then I can pretend to listen while I doze off every now and then."

Sly was turning over his list of excuses to avoid the meeting. "I could claim I had contracted a most serious, exotic disease that afflicts only raccoons. I could call it Accoonarestia Mytoeache. That's Latino-Greek for an acute faux paw. That might do the trick." So Sly lumbered off to write a fake prescription for oxycodone with a note detailing that he would be confined to complete bed rest with the sole exception being time to gather food. "This oughtta do the trick," he boasted in a fleeting moment of glory and self-congratulation. Then as he set out paper and pen and practiced making illegible scrawls, he had second thoughts. "This won't work. Nobody gets sick in the second life. Phil will sit on me, literally. He can't kill me, but he can make life miserable for a while. Nope, the risk of getting caught in a lie outweighs the slim chance of success. Nope, I'll just have to grin and bear it. Besides, it's only for half an hour, maybe an hour at the most. I might even try to pay attention. That'll make the time pass faster."

Carrie soared over the convocation area majestically for ten minutes before swooping down in the center, perhaps six feet away from where Phil would position himself. She had accepted the certainty of the meeting just as stoically as she had accepted every other episode of her assigned life. "Meetings, taxes, and death—no one can escape all three," Carrie concluded.

Amanda stepped into the meeting area briskly as if she were a competitor in some AKC competition. "Pete, come on over to the center of the circle so we can see and hear you better."

"Nobody wants to hear what I want to say," Pete moaned.

"Well, how can you be so sure?"

"I just know, Amanda. That's the way it is. Sly will make fun of me and no one will listen to me."

"I don't think Phil would allow that behavior. He just lets Sly play a little before he tugs on his leash of authority. Come on over."

"Well, if you insist, I will. Then you won't bother me? No barks, no growls, no bites?"

"None at all."

So Pete scurried over. Sly watched in fascination. "I never knew 'possums could run so fast," he confessed.

"There's a lot you don't know about opossums, my friend. For a short distance, we can run with the best."

"Except you can't outrun a car," Sly muttered under his breath.

Sensing the simmering hostility between Sly and Pete, Amanda decided to change the topic. "Well, I for one think these meetings are great."

Both Sly and Pete looked sideways at her with their eyes opened wide in disbelief. Even Carrie flapped her wings at this comment. In chorus, both Pete and Sly asked in bewildered tones, "And why is that, Amanda?"

"Because in our first lives, humans ruled. They led dogs around on leashes, gave us the food they wanted to give us, and ordered us around. And the humans didn't just lord it over dogs. They thought they were the top of the line and could do whatever they wanted with us animals. Some would even make jokes about the 'roadkill' lying in the streets." The last statement enlivened Carrie who took off for a brief flight. "They ruled over us and pretty well determined our first life. Now with these meetings we get to judge them."

"Whatever comes around, goes around," Carrie squawked as she soared overhead.

Phil made his majestic way towards the four. "I'm glad you're all here and here on time. "We can accomplish our mission if we focus. If we focus well, we can do all we're supposed to do in half an hour. Today, we're going to focus on five different themes."

"That means about six minutes each, right, boss?"

"That's right, Carrie, but only if we focus. If we get too off-track, the meeting might last a lot longer." Here Phil shot an accusing glare at both Sly and Pete, who for the moment, at least, yielded to Phil's wishes. "We're going to examine his early school year days, just focusing on these themes: 1) ambivalence towards war; 2) Ambivalence towards religion; 3) respect for education; 4) respect towards animals; 5) admiration for athletic accomplishments."

"Phil, that's a lot to look at," Pete protested.

"That's why we need to get to work right away. Carrie, start keeping time."

"Six minutes each, right?"

"Right you are." Then Phil thumped his chest and began his summary. "Even though Tom's Dad didn't want to have anything to do with war, Tom was taken in by all the television shows, movies, and along with his friends, the comic books, all presenting war as a heroic enterprise. In a vacant lot near their neighborhood, they would sometimes play act their heroic deaths. 'Yankee dog,' you die,' exploded the speaker tag in one of their favorite comic books. Tom and his friends would practice dying a perfect death if there is such a thing. Tom and three of his friends would form a single-file line and march up a hill—actually it was just a minor mound about eight feet high. There, one-by-one they'd collapse onto the earth, whispering, 'Give this to ma, would ya," to the boy behind him. Then in each rehearsed death, they'd slowly turn to one side, and expire with eyes closed solemnly. Other times, they'd storm this same mound, which they called Pork Chop Hill, a name they stole from a movie and, in John Wayne fashion, rout the invisible enemy from the mound, screaming, 'Take this, you Commie bastard.' The Korean War was still fresh in their minds because of the comic books they read and treasured, so they chose the Commies as their target. Besides, one of the boys had a father who had fought in World War II—on the German side."

"'Dulce et decorum est pro patria mori,' concluded Sly.

"What's that, Sly, some kind of raccoon lingo?" Pete asked.

"No, 'possum, it's Latin, from one of Horace's poems. Then a British soldier used the maxim ironically in one of his poems. It means, 'Sweet and fitting is it to die for the fatherland.'"

"Sometimes the carrion is sweet but never the dying. That's why we carrion feeders wait until death has come in all of its gruesome finality."

"I never knew you read poetry, Sly," Amanda added.

"Yeah, well, sometimes I get bored washing my hands so then I take out a book. I've been reading a lot lately. I've been playing around with the idea of composing an ode to a treed raccoon. It would be a first-person account, of course. Here the first couple of lines:

> 'Oh, racy, ravenous, raucous raccoon
> What prompts you high to challenge the moon?
> Is it the horrid humans hunting you down?
> Or do you love being the clever clown.'
> I haven't finished the remaining forty-eight lines, but I'm
> working on it as we speak."

Pete had had enough of Sly's versification, so he changed the topic. "I heard that Army food isn't that great. Sometimes an opossum won't even touch it. So, what's with the glorifying of war, Phil? Are humans that stupid?"

"If it weren't for all the propaganda, pomp, and circumstance, who would enlist to fight?" Phil commented.

"I bet they've got a pack mentality. They want to protect their territory, their bones, and their food, so they bark at any and all who come near. Then the other packs start barking and growling and then comes the yipping and biting. Soon it's just all a bloody mess." Amanda added.

"With all that time spent fighting, how do they get food?" Pete wondered.

"They steal it from their enemies and call it spoils of war," Sly intoned.

"Do they like their food spoiled?" Carrie wondered.

"Carrie, I said spoils, not spoiled." Sly explained, quite exasperated.

"I didn't know there was a difference," Carrie said. "But we don't have much more time on this topic. What did Tom's father say about these war games?"

"He dismissed them as boyish fantasies," Phil said. "But the media then—television, film, comic books, Memorial Day rhetoric— all presented war as the inevitable march of American triumph and the glorious, pretty much pain-free death of only a few American soldiers. But then Tom's Dad would have a most inglorious epileptic seizure and so as a young boy Tom didn't know whom to believe—his own eyes or the eyes of all those around him. Back then, no one knew or at least no one talked about the suffering of the wounded, disabled soldiers who felt the pain of war long after the peace treaties were signed."

"Time's almost up for this theme."

"All right, Carrie, we can move onto the next one," Phil realized that Amanda would empathize with the plight of a conflicted boy; he also knew that Sly for all of his narcissism and apparent amorality intellectually abhorred war as a pointless exercise in self-destruction. Pete had sensed that with war comes starvation and, quite likely disease. Carrie viewed war as a necessary—at least, for her species—but hellish reality. Sly, too, observed that the old men who started wars needed lots of young men to die in them.

"When Tom wasn't out playing war hero/ martyr, he attended school and did homework and a little light reading on his own," Phil continued, changing topics. Inwardly, he moaned, for he feared that war, which permeated all of human history, would continue its death march. He also knew that the devastation of war affected all animals as well, for he had witnessed the devastation wrought by war on his own species. So, Phil changed topics not only in the interest of time but also out of his own distress. "Tom studied hard. He'd walk the mile home from school and then break out his books. He studied to please his parents, but he also studied to please himself. And here it's fair to say that Tom had a younger brother and sister. In his early years, he pleased his parents by playing mini-parent with his younger siblings. Of course, he experienced the usual sibling rivalry, but his brother entered the family when Tom was six and already in kindergarten, and his sister came two years later. In kindergarten, Tom relished all the attention he received from his fellow students when he told them and his teacher about his baby brother. He told each of them about how he had held his brother and helped out his mother. His teacher lavished praise on Tom for being such a good brother. Sibling rivalry had not yet set in although it would appear later. Tom found himself the toast of kindergarten even though he hadn't mastered the art of drawing perfectly in lines or cutting a straight edge. Like many other boys, Tom would refine his fine motor skills later in life. He studied hard and paid heed to his mother's advice: 'I can understand why you might have trouble with a certain subject or skill. I can't understand not trying your best. That's unacceptable.' Even in kindergarten, Tom realized that he wasn't the best artist and his scissors frequently followed more of a zigzag pattern than a straight line. Still, he excelled in reading, for his parents had given him a head start."

"Yeah, yeah, OK, Phil, I get it. In fact we all do. So the kid tried hard to do well in school and liked reading. So what? Lots of kids are like that. So, what's the big deal? He was a good boy, so let's give him a gold star and move on." Sly was bored and didn't hesitate to voice his boredom.

"Sly, I bet his kindergarten teacher was glad to have Tom in his class. You know a lot of human children aren't that fortunate to have loving parents who value education." Amanda was scolding Sly. He turned away from her and raised his upper lip in scorn.

Pete had listened carefully. "Did Tom get any treats for trying hard in school?" he wondered.

"A few, especially at report card time," Phil responded.

"Yeah, it always helps to sweeten the pot a little," Pete added.

"So, the kid was leading a fairytale life, and life was a breeze, so what!" Sly spat out the words in contempt.

"It wasn't all fairytale happy, Sly. You forget that in the hierarchy of status for boys what counts does not occur in the classroom." Phil didn't want to come across as some pedantic pedagogue nor as some kind of Zen master, but he did speak definitively.

"Yeah, so what does matter, o g—" Sly caught himself. He realized that he had crossed the line. He was about to add sarcastically, "o, great one," but stopped short of open defiance.

"Sly, as you probably know, what does matter for boys of Tom's age, is not performance in the classroom but on the playing field. Saturday mornings meant soccer games, and the talk of schoolyard centered on who did what in those games."

"Yeah, I guess I can see that. I'm sorry, Phil. I guess I jumped the gun." Sly apologized—this time sincerely.

"Tom's soccer coach also was the father of one of the boys on the team. One of the perks for a volunteer coach is being able to coach your own child. For some, this job presents a challenge. A coach is supposed to be impartial and judge matters like playing time and position objectively. Many a parent / coach has agonized over such matters. But for a few, there's no challenge at all. When you have authority, you use it and use it to your own advantage they argued. So, the son of the coach would be a star, and father / coach would see to it that his dreams of athletic gory would be played out vicariously by the triumphs of his son. To accomplish that goal, the father / coach organized his playbook and practice time around the focal point of his coaching philosophy—making his son the star. And star status was conferred on those who scored goals. This coach relegated all those whom he deemed as non-athletes—that is, those who did well in school and didn't trash talk— to defensive positions, where in his playbook they'd never have a chance at scoring a goal. Tom fell into this category and played every game with the same enthusiasm as he displayed at school. But he enjoyed no accolades—except from his father. It also didn't help that Tom's father never joined the post-game beer bashes with some of the other fathers. Because of his seizure medication, he couldn't drink, and there were other reasons. He didn't want Tom growing up equating playing sports with getting trashed in some drinking binge, and he had work to do at home. As a result, in the playground on the Monday following Saturday's game or sometimes games, Tom and six other boys felt isolated. They even started to separate themselves from the designated stars and formed their own little group to play impromptu hoc-soc games." Here, Phil closed his book of notes and looked at his four colleagues. "You know, guys, I did my share of chest thumping during my days on earth, and sometimes you've just got to do it just to make your voice heard. But it can be overdone."

"You're right, Phil. Sometimes I had to bark and growl and play a role as some vicious attack dog. It's just the way it is with humans, dogs, and just about all animals." Amanda was trying to console Phil as she sensed he was feeling a bit contrite for past indiscretions. "It's the way of the flesh."

"So, Phil, what's wrong with a little drinking?" Pete asked. "I mean I've taken a sip or two from some cast-off beer bottle and the stuff tastes pretty good." Pete looked around at his colleagues for support.

Sly seconded Pete's point.

"You're right about that, Pete." Phil responded, surprising them all who just assumed he was a total teetotaler. "Back in my glory days, my keeper would share a Budweiser with me at the end of the day. Of course six ounces of beer wouldn't do much to a 776 pound body, but it tasted great on one of those steaming hot August days in the Midwest. I can still taste it now. Ah, Budweiser." He paused a bit in nostalgic revelry. "It's just that all good things can be overdone."

"Yeah, Phil, one time I gorged myself on a peck of peaches, and just about blew my insides out," Pete recalled.

"Yeah, and one time I ate three chocolate bars that were left on the table," Amanda added.

Carrie and Sly looked on in agreement but didn't say anything. Sly was worried that the meeting would go overtime and Carrie wanted to move on so that the meeting wouldn't go overtime.

Phil knew it was time to move on. "Tom knew he was considered to be no athlete by the powers that be, but he always found himself yearning for some athletic glory."

"It's time to get to the next topic," Carrie commented blandly.

"So it is," Phil determined. "In addition to schooling, soccer, and his daily family life, Tom also immersed himself in one other major activity."

"Eating," Pete said "There's nothing better than peanut butter and jelly between two slices of white bread or noodles lathered in butter. That's the stuff that kids like, so do opossums, that is when we're not out foraging in the wild for persimmons and wild blackberries. And anything else we can get our paws on."

Sly shot Pete a look whose meaning screamed to all there that Pete was an idiot. Even Amanda, turned her head away in bewilderment and thought to herself, "How could Pete say that?" Carrie just noted the time.

Stroking his chin to keep himself from shooting back some sarcastic remark, Phil then spoke in a calm voice without a hint of scathing sarcasm.

"It's true, Pete, that many human children love their peanut butter and jelly sandwiches. Some even top them off with sliced bananas. Others subsist on their buttered noodles, but we'll just note those down as part of the human diet. No, the other theme of note to us concerns the spiritual dimension."

"I think Phil's talking about religion, Pete, in case you didn't get it."

Trying to recapture some sense of dignity, Pete responded in the most scholarly voice he could muster. "Human children are not developmentally ready to address the domain of the spirit world."

"I'm not so sure you're right, Pete," Amanda stated. "Children are often more attuned to the spirit world than are adult humans. They live in a world where fairytales have meaning and address their fears and loves and hopes and desires. For them Santa Claus has meaning as the spirit of giving. Of course, they view themselves as the main beneficiaries of that Santa Claus spirit. Sometimes they speak with the angels and their parents don't know it. They love fairy gardens because the fairies reflect the natural world, at least that part that isn't savage. Adults get so caught up in meeting their needs and lusts for food and security and sex and power that they forget that childhood world of spirits and fairies. These adult humans often live in a world of gluttony, lust, and pride as they forget the spiritual world of their childhood."

"And sometimes religion loses its connection to that spiritual world and becomes simply the celebration of the cultural world of adults. Religion and culture entangle themselves so tightly that sometimes religion loses its spirit and simply finds itself reflecting the dominant culture. That is why saints throughout the ages, ones like St. Francis of Assisi—who also loved animals as you recall—have had to bring religion back to its meaningful roots."

"Ah, religion is just the intoxicant of the masses. It makes people toe the line and obey the commands of the rich and powerful and the rich and powerful want to keep things just the way they are." Sly spoke bitterly.

"Then, Sly, what are we doing here?" Phil retorted.

Sly grumbled a bit, but Phil resumed. "There's some truth in what all of you have said, but it may take a while to sort things out. As Amanda said, children often do intuitively sense the spiritual. As Pete mentioned, for many food is a higher priority than the spiritual, especially for those not just a little hungry but actually starving. And, Sly has a point, too.

Religion can just find itself as a reflection of the dominant culture. But, for Tom at a young age, religion gave him some sense of order. He prayed before he went to sleep and when he woke up. Sometimes, he'd mumble his prayers away so he could tear into his meal and then rush out to play. On weekends, he'd play soccer in the morning and early afternoon and then go to five o'clock mass later on. Sundays meant sleeping in and having a big breakfast. He folded his hands reverently when he made his First Communion and envisioned himself as one of God's soldiers when he made his Confirmation. But he felt most at ease when he slipped into an empty church, when all was quiet and lightly lit with flickering candles. He'd look up at the large crucifix behind the altar and wonder, if he, too, would be called to suffer and die and then be reborn into a new life."

"I'd like to know, Phil, just what was this Tom kid doing being in an empty church all by himself? It seems more than a little whacko to me," Sly asked.

"A good question, Sly." Phil stared at Sly calmly. "Tom was replacing the candles that had burned all their wax with new candles."

"So, was he getting paid to do this or had he just been brainwashed into thinking that he was doing God's work by being a candle boy?"

"Not either one, Sly. His religion teacher offered him the job because he had already learned his catechism well. Tom like the chance to get up and do something rather than sit in a desk reciting answers he already knew. You see, for Tom, religion was just another subject at school, like math or reading. He learned it all well because that's what his parents and teachers expected him to do."

"Yeah, if say so, Phil. I think this Tom guy is just some kind of goodie-two-shoes who needs to get his butt kicked so he knows how the world really operates." Sly spit out these words vehemently.

"That will come, Sly, that will come." Phil almost whispered mournfully.

"Time's up," Carrie shrieked.

"All right, Carrie, there's just one more them we need to address before we adjourn."

"What's that, Phil?" Amanda asked enthusiastically.

"Well, none of us may like this one very much, but we need to address it. As you know, Tom's parents had done all they could do to foster a love of reading and Tom loved to escape into a book and wonder at worlds unfamiliar to him. As a boy, he read book after book about the American frontier and mountain men and woodcraft and Native Americans and—"

"I know what's coming next," Sly interrupted: trapping and the fur trade."

"You're right," Phil remarked. "Tom loved reading about early America, and a lot of the history of early America centered on the fur trade, and St. Louis was the center of that trade. At first, Tom was content with just the vicarious thrill of imagining himself a frontiersman and trapper. He had gone camping with his Scout group and loved it. One elderly Scout leader showed the boys how to make a fire during a rain storm, how to make the best lean-to's, how to fish without a rod and reel, how to gig frogs, in the summer, and snare rabbits in the winter, how to identify animals by their tracks, how to cook over an open fire without burning yourself. and a host of other practical skills. And Tom was hooked. He longed to skill himself in frontier ways. Then, when he got back from Scout camp, several boys a few years older than he was bragged about how they could earn money trapping and selling the pelts. He was enthralled. So, he saved money earned from doing odd jobs around the neighborhood—cutting grass, raking leaves, and picking peaches for one old man who still operated a small orchard in the sprawling suburb of cookie-cutter suburban houses— went to the hardware store, bought some steel, leg hold traps. In early fall, he boiled these traps in hickory nuts and then buried them to remove human scent."

"Yeah, that doesn't work too well," Sly interrupted. "I can smell human no matter how much they try to cover up their stink. There's no good coming from their trapping ways."

"Hey, Sly, Pete countered. "I've seen you trap fish and crawdads and then eat them up," Pete answered. "It's just he way of nature."

"Well, when I do it, it's different. I'm trapping to stay alive. That kid was trapping just to live out some fantasy."

Phil looked at the two feuding colleagues. Before he could say anything, Amanda broke in the conversation. "Well, I used to chase rabbits and squirrels in my former life. I even chased a raccoon once, but they all got away. I think maybe Pete's right about its being part of nature and that Sly's right about not killing for just sport or to fulfill some fantasy."

Then Phil settled matters. "Let me finish. Tom was just a boy then, and boys need to learn and sometimes the only way they can learn is from experience. Don't judge until I finish this episode in Tom's tale." Phil looked around. Carrie added that they only had a few more minutes to meet, that is unless Phil needed more time. That last comment sealed their lips. Phil continued. "As I was saying, Tom was all ready to trap once the cold weather of November set in. So, when his family set out for a weekend visit to his uncle's farm, Tom asked if he could set out his traps. His uncle allowed him but only if he set them farther out so he wouldn't hurt any of the local dogs who sometimes strayed onto his farm. Tom agreed and added that he would set his traps only at the distant corners of his uncle's farm, where domestic animals didn't wander. He carefully set his traps while his father looked on with mixed feelings. He was proud that his son had taken initiative and tried to train himself but remained skeptical about the outcome. Tom set his traps carefully, wearing gloves that he had buried for weeks to remove the human smell, set them so that all the steel lay hidden, and then baited them with small cuts of sardines."

"Yeah, well, I guess the kid isn't that dumb. There isn't a raccoon alive that can resist the smell of sardines, and that smell can spread a mile." Sly, as usual, couldn't contain himself.

Phil looked up indulgently and then continued. "So, the traps were laid, and Tom waited until just after sunrise to check them. He got up, threw his clothes on and set out with his father, who carried an ancient .22 rifle inherited from his own father. It took father and son half an hour to trudge out to where the traps were laid. Tom had even drawn a rough diagram of where he had set each of his six traps. The first two weren't sprung but the sardine bait was missing. Then father and son walked over carefully to the third one, which lay by a stream at the base of a willow. Tom looked on in fascination. A burly raccoon, fattened by autumn's bounty, scented the sardine and then ever so carefully set his paw underneath the pan of the trap, skillfully without any downward pressure at all, snatched the bait and then tossed it into his mouth before turning towards the astounded humans and giving them satisfied grin that seemed to say, 'You can't beat me.' Tom's father turned to his son and just said, 'I guess he outsmarted us.' Tom agreed. He found his remaining traps also unsprung and devoid of their bait. He collected his traps and gave them to his uncle."

"So, what's your point, Phil?" Sly smirked.

"Tom had learned to respect the intelligence of that raccoon and of all animals. He was learning to value the gifts of all of God's creation."

"Well, maybe I was a little too quick to judge the guy," Sly confessed.

Pete saw a chance to school his colleague and couldn't waste the opportunity. "Yeah, Sly, don't judge others so that they won't judge you." Sly just threw him a sneer with an upturned lip and eyes askance.

Amanda added, "Boys can be so cruel and so sweet at the same time."

Carrie concluded the meeting with a simple, "Time's up."

STAGE THREE

GROWING GAINS AND PAINS

"Tom turned twelve," Phil intoned.

"Oh, come on, Phil, are we gonna have to hear about some kind of bizarre human rite of passage or something like that?" Sly spat out his distaste for the weekly meeting.

"Yeah," Pete seconded Sly's distaste. "I mean I was havin' a nice sleep and here I had to get up and scurry on over to this stupid convocation area and listen to this garbage about some 'tween human, not a kid any more, not an adult, not even what do they call 'em, yeah, a teenager."

"What else more pressing do you have to do?" Amanda asked. "It's not like you're doing anything worthwhile. Phil is giving us a chance we never had in the before life, an opportunity to evaluate a human and pass our findings on. I think it's a grand opportunity. The after life ought to be more meaningful than just an endless round of eating and sleeping."

Then Carrie weighed in with the deciding factor. "All of this fussing and feuding just prolongs the meeting. Phil's the referee and timekeeper, and he'll just add on time, right, Phil."

"Right you are, Carrie," Phil concluded. He turned his massive head towards Sly and Pete and stared at them. Then he coolly added. "Of course, the after life does include other options, rather less appealing than the ones you currently enjoy."

This comment silenced any dissent. "Let's go. We have a job to do, and we need the insight of everyone. Sly, what do you think of Tom's attitude towards animals?"

"Well, at our last session, I figured that the kid Tom would turn out just as some kind of sadistic trophy trapper, but I guess he learned that we raccoons can be more crafty than humans. So, I guess the kid is headed in the right direction."

"Yeah," Pete added. "I don't see this kid as turning out to be one of those humans who go out of their way to hurt animals. When the kid becomes old enough to drive, I don't see him going out of his way to smash some opossum just crossing the road. So, I've got to give the kid some credit, something I rarely do for a human. So far, I guess he's all right."

"You know, we're all hunters in our own sort of way. It's part of nature." Amanda paused and then continued. "I'd love to catch a tasty rabbit, and, Sly, you've been known to sample a delicious crawdad or two."

"So I have, Amanda. "So I have." Sly was smug and almost boasting.

"I think what is missing is the spiritual element." Amanda commented.

"You're not gonna go all religious on us and start preaching, are you, Amanda?" Pete added as he slowly munched on a marshmallow.

"Well, some human hunters would pray after a kill. Some Native Americans would even apologize for the kill, which was necessary for their life even if it meant the end of another life. Nature can be very cruel, you know. And if there's pleasure in some things, there's pain in others. There's a cycle of life and death."

"That's why Tom at age twelve experiences both growing gains and pains." Phil wanted the group to get back on topic. Carrie started her timer. "Tom had a big growth spurt. Suddenly, he was taller and stronger than almost any of the boys at his school. Even the soccer coach who had favored his son over Tom and everybody else noticed this growth. Tom was still playing defense but now he had opportunities to score. In one league game, Tom took the ball at midfield, turned and noted that the goalkeeper had positioned himself at the edge of the penalty box, far from the goal line. So Tom slammed a shot from midfield, and the ball screamed past the amazed goalie, who just stared, open-eyed, in bewilderment. Tom's team won that game, 1-0, and for a brief moment Tom enjoyed hero status, something he had never felt before. But that euphoria turned out to be short-lived. The win sent the team into the City / County championship. The final game would be played in early December. The weather shifted from the cool, invigorating breezes of autumn to the cold, paralyzing blasts of winter. Tom's team would be playing the defending champions, and the boys on Tom's team—and the coach as well—had pinned their hopes on their new hero—Tom. Tom had to mark the best player in the county, maybe the best in the state, Tony Anselmo. Ten minutes into the game, Tom dogged Tony Anselmo as he tried to dribble downfield. He forced Tony back past the midfield line, deep into his own territory. But then Tony passed to one of his fullbacks, raced across field to the other side, took a pass. Tom found himself way out of position, so he tried to do what his coach had told him—mark Tony Anselmo one-on-one. But doing so left Tom's side of the field wide open. Tony faked a run down the opposite side and then deftly passed the ball to one of his teammates on the open side. Completely unmarked, the opposing player drilled the ball into the net. Even though he had followed, his coach's instructions, even though the great Tony Anselmo didn't score, Tom's team had lost. And Tom felt that just as his teammates had pinned all their hopes on him, now they laid all the blame on him. Tom didn't take much comfort when his dad told him, 'Good game.' He felt that the words ringed hollow. He left the field almost on the verge of crying as the victory chants of the opposing team echoed in his ears."

"So, Phil, is Tom learning that a lot of time life is more about losing and coping with loss than it is about winning?" Amanda asked.

"Yeah, and there's something else, too," Sly added. "This Tom kid is learning that sometimes the adults aren't always right."

Pete asked, "Did Tom get a treat after the game?"

"Yes, Pete, Tom's Dad took him out for a consolation chocolate shake."

"I've tasted those, at least I tasted a few drops from some discarded paper cup. Those chocolate shakes are good stuff." Pete looked around for support.

"Yeah, Pete, they're good," Sly seconded.

"Time's up. We need to move on to another topic," Carrie stated, focusing on her watch.

Phil hadn't quite finished his discussion of Tom's soccer experiences, so he devised another way to continue the topic without significantly circumventing his own rules. "In school, Tom continued to be an exemplary student except in art and music. He still couldn't cut a straight line and his drawings could be described as primitive at best. In music, his voice started changing at a relatively early age, and he was granted a reprieve from choir practice. In fact, his choir instructor told him directly not to sing and not to show up for the ten am high mass, where the church choir featured prominently in the liturgy. Tom was happy because he didn't like church pomp very much and the sweet smell of incense sickened him like a Halloween excess of candy. So, he preferred the stark simplicity of the earlier masses, so did the rest of his family, and that family was growing. Tom now had a brother six years younger than himself and a sister eight years younger. So, as the elder brother, Tom felt it his duty to instruct his younger siblings in all matters not officially on the school or parental syllabus."

"Phil, I gotta say something, if you don't mind," Sly interrupted. I was thinking about it, and I was finding this Tom kid a little too much. You know a goodie two shoe type who was good at everything. I was glad to learn he had some shortcomings. I guess his fine motor skills just weren't that good. Now me, I've got highly developed fine motor skills."

"Yeah, Sly, you can pick two ounces of tossed out sardines from a two ton dumpster," Pete interjected.

"Hey, those are survival skills, and highly honed skills at that," Sly countered.

Wanting the discussion to get back on topic, Amanda asked, "So how did Tom get along with his siblings? That's really important."

"Thanks, Amanda, for getting us back on topic," Phil responded, casting a sidelong look at Sly and Pete. "He got along pretty well. Oh, at first there was some jealously when his younger brother was born and garnered everyone's attention, but at six years older and in his own mind at least that much wiser, Tom thought it his duty to teach his brother all of the unofficial rules of conduct."

"What were the names of his younger siblings?" Amanda asked.

"Pete and Grace," Phil stated.

"Hey, so Tom named his younger bro after me," Pete said, half-joking. "For humans to bestow my humble name on their child is an honor to me and an honor to them and to their child."

"Tom was named after an uncle, and so was Pete. Grace got her name from an aunt." Phil replied dryly.

"Well, it's still an honor," Pete added.

Shaking his head, Phil resumed. "So, Tom thought he had the duty to teach Pete all the playground rules he had had to learn the hard way. First of all, he practiced soccer skills, especially goal-scoring skills with young Pete. Tom didn't want his younger brother to play in the obscurity of the back line. He wanted him front and center as the star of the six- year- old squad."

"Did Tom succeed?' Amanda asked.

"No, the coach of the sixers as they were called played his son as striker and moved young Pete to the back line, where Tom had played in obscurity for the first few years of his athletic life. Actually, that placement may have been serendipitous, for, like his older brother, Pete was a natural defender."

"Ok, Phil, you got me," Pete the opossum interrupted. "So what does that weird word sere-end-piteous mean?"

"Sort of like lucky, right?" Carrie cawed.

"Right," Phil exclaimed, a bit surprised by the usually taciturn Carrie's interjection. "Tom also explained to his brother that first grade would be a lot tougher than kindergarten, so Pete better be ready for some tough work. 'Of course,' Tom pontificated, 'first grade is not near as hard as seventh. That's when the homework starts piling up.'"

"Tom also guided his siblings on tours of the zoo, which had started to make some changes, and all of them were starting to show a new regard and respect for the dignity of the animals. Of course, by that time I had already passed on, so Tom could only provide a little vicarious experience of my exploits."

"There you go again, Phil. So what's with this vike-ari-us stuff?" Pete interrupted.

"It means 'experienced or realized through imaginative or sympathetic participation in the experience of another,' you slothful twit. Pete, you'd know this stuff if you didn't spend all of eternity hanging in a tree and sleeping." Sly complained.

"Well, excuse me, Mr. Dictionary, or should I just call you Mr. Dick?" Pete retorted.

Phil had had it. He started his chest thumping and that at least quieted down the two. "If you two don't stop this endless bickering, you might find yourselves somewhere else for all of eternity."

"Sorry," Pete squeaked in a high-pitched whisper.

"Yeah, sorry, boss," Sly added in a low- pitched bass whisper.

"All right, now this next section is important," Phil cautioned. "So, listen carefully and think before you speak."

"Yes, boss," Sly and Pete said in concert.

"Tom had always regarded his religion as a given. He went to mass weekly, received communion, said his morning, evening, and mealtime prayers. He went with his class to do volunteer work at the Ronald McDonald House, where he did the dishes and helped out families who had a child in long-term hospital care. He took his position as oldest sibling seriously."

"You mean like when he coached his younger brother Pete on how to be the star soccer player of the six –year- old team?" Pete the possum interjected.

"That's right, Pete. He also tried to map out the unwritten playground rules for him."

Sly pricked up his ears at this. "So what kind of unwritten laws are we talking about?"

"From what I understand," Phil responded, "things like which spaces on the playground were reserved for certain grades. The eighth graders, for instance, claimed exclusive rights to the basketball court, kindergarteners were expected to stay on the small climbing apparatus and swings. The rest of the playground was unofficially divvied up for each of the grades. The teachers didn't direct this. It was just determined by a silent, unwritten consensus."

"I understand perfectly," Amanda added. "Like canines, humans are pack animals. And the pack has certain rules of conduct, never written but occasionally challenged, like when two dogs vie for the top spot. And everybody knows when that battle is coming. Sometimes for humans the unwritten laws are more important than the written ones. That's odd because humans pride themselves so much on their written laws and constitutions."

"Well said, Amanda, and that leads to my next point." Phil fingered through the first volume of Tom's life, trying to find the exact passage. "Ah, here it is. As I mentioned earlier, Tom had always taken his religion as a given just as he had always taken his parents as a given. But then in eighth grade, he learned that some of his friends had parents who were divorcing. This shook his faith. He didn't understand. 'Weren't father and mother supposed to stay together for life.' Tom was perplexed and upset. 'What would I do if my parents divorced? They seemed happy, but so did his friend's mom and dad. Jim never talked of his parents quarreling or anything. Just one day they called him to the kitchen and explained that Jim's dad would be moving out.' Tom worried that the same scene would play out for him. 'It's not fair. It's not right. This is not the way it's supposed to be,' he cried out inwardly. He watched his own mother's and father's every move. They didn't act angry or anything. In fact, they seemed to be just the way they always had been. But so did Jim's parents. So, for months Tom eyed his parents suspiciously, still trying to detect any hint of divorce. He didn't see any. Still he remained wary."

"So did his mom and dad split?" Sly asked rather flippantly.

"No, Sly, they didn't."

"I figured. This is some kind of La-La story where everything comes out just peachy."

"Well, we'll see about that." Phil replied. "Tom's tale, like that of many other humans has its twists and turns."

"Yeah, well, my tail has twists and turns, too. See the black and brown bands?"

"You're wasting time, Sly," Carrie cautioned, flapping her wings—and that seldom was a good sign.

Sly retreated into silence.

Phil resumed. "Just when it seemed that Tom's doubts about his parents' relationship had ended, another troubling event shook Tom's confidence in the stability of life." Sly checked himself from blurting out any snide comment, so Phil resumed—but only after giving Sly a fixed stare. "The assistant parish priest had taught Tom's religion class. This priest was young, popular, and a favorite of the children. They affectionately called him Father Mojo, for luck and God's favor seemed to be with him. Then, shocking Tom and everyone else in the parish, this priest announced that he was leaving the priesthood and marrying a former nun. He omitted the part about the nun's being pregnant. But the rumors flew fast and furious as a spring thunderstorm. Tom was shaken, first by the prospect of divorce and then by this scandalous marriage. He stopped going to Confession and wanted to forego weekly mass. He withdrew a bit from his teachers and became cynical although he still enjoyed the intellectual challenges of learning."

"I feel sorry for Tom," Amanda confessed. "Everything had been going so well. Life seemed to be operating in an orderly, reasonable routine. The world seemed to make sense. It's hard. I remember one of my canine friends whose kindly human passed on, and then the pup found herself at the mercy of a stingy new owner who fed her little and beat her often. It's enough to make you want to die."

"Unfortunately, Amanda, things got worse before they got better. Tom was feeling estranged from his own parents. Let me recount a scene between Tom and his Dad. I'll read from the book so I won't omit anything. Here goes—

'Tom, you need to clean up your room.'

'I'll get to it when I want to.'

'You'll do it now. You've already put it off all week.'

'You can't tell me what to do. You're no better than the rest of them.'

"Who are the them you're talking about, Tom?'

'You know, that pervert Father M- and Jim's parents. I can't believe it.'

Tom's father had spoken brusquely, for he assumed he was dealing with only adolescent petulance. Now he realized there were deeper issues.

'Tom, he world's a crazy place and people—all people—do stupid things from time to time. I've had more than my share of dumb decisions. We try to learn from them and not judge others too sharply.'

Still reeling from the blows to his security and worldview, Tom kept up the cynical tone. 'Yeah, well, I hear it's worse than just stupid mistakes. My buddies have been talking about some priest up in Florissant who likes little boys, if you know what I mean. They're all sick, and I'm sick of them.'

'Tom, all of us, men and women, boys and girls, are sinners alike. All we can do is to ask forgiveness and try to learn from our mistakes. The principles aren't wrong, but sometimes we humans pervert the principles. You know the Our Father?"

'You've got to be kiddin', Dad. I've been rattlin' that off since I was younger than my kid sister, little Gracie.'

'Towards the end, the prayer goes *and forgive us our trespasses as we forgive those who trespass against us.*'

'Yeah, Dad, so what?'

'So what does that mean?'

'I dunno.'

'Yeah, you do. Think.'

'I guess we shouldn't judge others so that others and God, I guess, won't judge us. This is stupid, Dad. It sounds like religion class.'

'All right, let me put it this way. Do you remember last week's soccer game?'

'That's a dumb question. Of course, I do.'

'Do you recall that play towards the end of the first half when you got out of position and overcommitted so that the winger made an easy cross to the striker.'

'Yeah, and then our goalkeeper made an awesome save.'

'But, what if he hadn't?'

'Everybody would've blamed me.'

'So, by luck and your keeper's skill, you dodged a bullet. What did you do the rest of the game?'

'Stayed in my position and fell back, trying to cut the angle, not giving away any easy passes.'

'Isn't that what your coach told you to do at halftime?'

'Well, yeah, it was, but what does this have to do with Jim's parents and that Father M-pervert?'

'We all make mistakes, sometimes little ones and sometimes big ones. The world is far from perfect. All we can do sometimes is to ask for forgiveness and try not to make the same mistake over and over again.'

'You mean like when you leave the dome light on all night and the battery goes dead? That drives Mom crazy.'

'Yeah, that and other things. Anyway, clean up your room and make your Mom happy.'

Phil looked up from the heavy volume he was holding. Amanda had paid attention. Her head was upright and she gazed directly at Phil. Carrie was looking at her watch, Pete had gone asleep, and Sly was playing some raccoon video game called Snatch the Fish. So, Phil decided to rattle his little convocation. "OK, we're going to have a little quiz. The sooner you answer the questions, the sooner we'll adjourn for the week. Here goes. Question One, why is Tom upset with Jim's parents?'

Sly looked away and tried to nudge Pete awake. Carrie just looked at her watch. Phil said nothing for ten seconds. Then he yawned and simply remarked, "We've got all of eternity to deal with this one." Sly glanced around to see if there was some place he could slink away to, but the Convocation area was deliberately designed to be open, with no convenient little cubby holes to retreat to. Phil paused again for another ten seconds. Then he asked Amanda to answer the question.

"Tom's upset because his friend's parents are divorcing and is secretly afraid that his parents will do the same." Amanda responded.

"And why is Tom upset with Father M?" Phil asked Pete.

"He gives long sermons? I don't know, Phil."

"Sly, what do you think?"

"About what?'

"Father M, why is Tom upset with him?"

"I like Pete's answer," he replied smugly.

"Sly, this isn't a matter of like / don't like. It's a matter of fact."

"Well, right now I'm a little short of facts."

"Then, I guess I'll have to read the whole story over." So, Pete excused Amanda and Carrie and told the whole episode over to Pete and Sly, pausing every few sentences to make sure they were paying attention. They did—at least as well as they could.

STAGE FOUR

NEW CHALLENGES AND EXPECTATIONS: ROMANTIC, RACIAL, AND INTELLECTUAL

"THAT SUMMER WAS A CHALLENGING one for Tom," so Phil began the fourth session.

Sly rubbed his forepaws together and belted out, "Now we're getting to the good stuff. Challenging is just another way of saying, 'That kid's gonna screw up.' And there's nothing I like better than a good screw up. I mean, it's the story of my life."

"I don't like this. I'd prefer things just to go slow and easy," Pete replied, darting his eyes about furtively, scanning the area for a nice tree to retreat to. I like things safe."

Carrie broke her normal taciturn ways. "As for me, at least in my former life, I feasted on major screw ups: traffic accidents, road kill, dumb stunts gone wrong, drunkenness, all the machinations of Nature and stupidity combined."

Amanda quietly added, "Let's just listen to hear what Phil has to say."

"Thank you, Amanda," Phil nodded in her direction. "As I was saying-" Here Phil paused and stopped himself from adding the customary expression, "Before I was rudely interrupted." He realized that this barb would catch nothing but ill will. "Besides," Phil reasoned as he turned over the thoughts in his mind, "there is a certain amount of truth in Sly's reaction. Without conflict and failure, there wouldn't be much of a story to tell. So, Sly's got a point, but only a portion of the truth of it all."

"Hey, Phil, did you doze off or somethin'? C'mon, let's get going. Carrie, are you watchin' the clock?"

"I always do," Carrie shot back.

"OK, so, Phil, let's get on with it."

Amanda just laid herself down on the soft turf and thought, "What did I do in my former life to deserve this?"

"All right, Carrie, you can start the clock now that the preliminaries are over." That was Phil's way of warning Sly and keeping him in check. Amanda sat up so she could listen more attentively. "First comes the good news for Tom. He had won a scholarship to the local Jesuit high school. That's the good news. The bad news is that the scholarship covered tuition but not books. So, Tom needed a job to pay for the textbooks for English, Latin, philosophy, algebra, introductory physics, history, and keyboarding. The books for English were all inexpensive paperbacks, so Tom's father joked that his son ought to major in English, because the textbooks for the other courses weren't cheap. If Tom were lucky and bought them early enough, he might be able to lay his hands on good, used copies. But everyone else in Tom's incoming high school class had the same idea, so there was no guarantee that he could get the used copies. So, Tom took the most reasonable course of action."

Sly was about to say something like, "Tom robbed the local gas station," but even he realized that this would sound flippant and foolish. So, for once, he wisely held his impulses back. Phil looked up from his book to register Sly's reaction. "So far, so good," Phil thought before he resumed his account. "A country club about five miles away but on a bus line, was advertising for busboys. Tom called and was told to come out right away because three of their busboys had quit. Tom took the bus to the entranceway of the country club and to worlds completely foreign to him. The first world consisted of gently rolling hills with neatly manicured lawns, the whole scene exuding the allure of comfortable lives gently rolling on from one round of golf to the next. Tom caught a glimpse of one of the boys he had met at the freshman orientation. He was putting on a green just about twenty yards from the road that wound its way in graceful curves to the clubhouse. This boy waved at Tom as he mistook him for a fellow member of this exclusive club. Tom waved back and checked in at the office. He had been told to wear black pants and a white shirt for work. Luckily Tom had both in his otherwise rather meager wardrobe. Nervously, he filled out the application form and took out his Social Security card and birth certificate. The secretary's eyes scanned over both documents officiously and told Tom to report downstairs and to use the staircase behind the kitchen."

"So, the kid's gotta work. Big deal. That's the way it is," Sly blurt out. "Everybody's gotta hustle for food, drink, and in this kid's case books. So, who cares?"

"I'll bet that that Tom guy wanted to sleep in," Pete said.

Phil just looked at his watch and nodded to Carrie. Both fully understood what that meant. Phil was adding on time to the thirty minute session that would end up lasting forty-five minutes or more if the pointless interruptions continued.

"What made this job unique was that it introduced Tom to two worlds. The first one I mentioned indirectly, a world of easy wealth and inherited money, a world of gently rolling hills and relaxation. The other world lay downstairs in the basement below the kitchen, a place where the timecards listed names like Moses, Abraham, Washington, Isaiah, and others both familiar and unfamiliar to Tom. He soon figured that had entered a world foreign to him. He was the only white worker on the staff. He didn't mind this kind of reverse integration. His father had black families over to the house and had led a neighborhood welcoming committee when a black family moved in. He did recall, though, that his father had formed this ad hoc committee because some in his neighborhood were circulating petitions that screamed out in bold letters, *Keep our Neighborhood White*. Tom hadn't understood the uproar. Some of his friends said that their parents might move because of the black family. They said their parents told them that the property values would go down. Tom's dad rallied another group of neighbors for the welcoming committee. In the end, the black family moved in, and there were no problems except for occasional grumblings from gritted mouths.

"Tom dutifully slid his timecard into the slot and punched the clock. He was told he'd work in the patio, not far from the swimming pool. There he met his immediate supervisor, Albert. Albert was a black, middle-aged man who had worked at the country club for fifteen years. He kept his job by playing a role he didn't like. He would pretend to be utterly subservient to the whims of the white country club members. Tom witnessed this scene at 11:30 that even for his immature mind encapsulated the little social drama that would play out at the country club every day. A circuit judge, whose name Tom never learned, brought his family to the patio in swimsuits still dripping wet from the pool. Albert told Tom to go inside and bring out a linen tablecloth and silverware for four. Perplexed, Tom nevertheless followed his orders. He set the table—Tom's mother had seen to it that he knew how to set the table and clear it off—and brought out menus. The Judge then escorted his wife and two children, one around ten years old, the other about eight, to the table. Here they studied the menus carefully, with the water from their wet suits still dripping on the linen tablecloth. After several minutes of intense scrutiny, the Judge then bellowed out, 'Four hamburger deluxes, all medium rare.' Albert carefully noted down the order, took it to the kitchen, and in a few minutes brought out the four hamburgers with French fries. As if he were sampling a rare wine, the Judge sniffed the hamburger, made a face, and took a tiny bite. 'This isn't medium rare. It's just barely beyond rare. Take it back to the kitchen.' Albert took it back while Tom took care of small orders for ice cream cones and sodas. Then Albert brought the burgers back. The Judge took a bite and then ruled that 'Now this is what medium rare means.' Albert later whispered to Tom that these were exactly the same hamburgers he had first brought out and that he had just taken them to the kitchen to keep them warm and the Judge happy."

"This whole scene stinks of a power trip to me," Sly pronounced.

"Yes," Amanda seconded Sly's view," just who does this judge fellow think he is?"

"Exactly what the young busboy thought," Phil continued. "Especially when he learned that the waiter he served under worked two jobs just to make ends meet."

"Well, I don't blame that Judge guy for wanting a nice hamburger after a swim, but that whole business about sending it back to the kitchen just seems like a big waste of time. Why the Judge could have taken four or five bites of the burger instead of killing time and sending it back." Pete squeaked out indignantly.

"In the end, we're all dead meat," pronounced Carrie.

"Well, things went from bad to worse. Tom felt that Albert, who had been accepting of him, really wasn't accepted by the Judge and his set, and the Judge was most visibly white and so was Tom. When business slackened a bit, Tom told Albert he was sorry for the way that Judge had treated him. Albert and Tom busied themselves by polishing silverware. Albert stopped momentarily and looked Tom in the eye. 'Hey, Tom, that Judge guy is a major jerk. You'll find that kind all over the place. Besides, he pays major bucks to lord it over waiters, busboys, and anybody else. Don't feel sorry for me. Feel sorry for the sorry guys who come before him in court.'

"Then to make matters even worse, a young girl who looked every bit the young woman, flung herself on top of the bar that had served as a buffer zone between the club's members and the club's workers. Her white bikini set off the bronzed complexion of her most gracefully curved torso. Even Tom realized that she was playing a game—look but don't touch. Still, Tom had to turn and hide the conspicuous erection that was stretching the boundary between prudence and desire. 'Well, I think it's shameful the way some white people treat blacks,' she said before jumping off the bar and heading back to the pool.

"'Man, that's some jailbait,' Albert commented as he was setting the table for a party of eight. Tom just exhaled, glad to return to the routine of work. He had never realized before how deep the racial divide was. He asked Albert how he put up with it. 'It's all part of a crazy game, Tom. I figure you don't know about it, do you?' Tom shook his head in response. 'This crazy shit's been going on for hundreds of years. It'll stop. It'll have to stop. Better sooner than later. A lot of folks can't wait any more.'

"Tom soon learned just how crazy the game had gotten. At three o'clock he headed down to the kitchen's basement that doubled as a storehouse and as the break room for the waiters, busboys and cooks and dishwashers. Tom's mom had fixed his a peanut butter and jelly sandwich and an apple and some homemade cookies for lunch. He sat down, happy to be off his feet for a short while and happy to be enjoying his favorite lunch. He hadn't noticed that his was the only white face there. Suddenly, Lamont, one of the barbeque cooks, slammed a knife into the wooden lunch table. Tom froze as he watched the blade still shaking from the impact.

"'Just what the hell is your white ass doin' down here?' Lamont demanded.

"'He's eating lunch just like the rest of us, Lamont. He's just a kid trying to earn a buck or two. Leave him be. He's not putting on any airs.' These words came from the aristocratically slender and sophisticated, Mr. Douglas Washington. His six foot-four frame towered over almost all of the people at the club, members and workers alike. In his case, the silver hair that graced his head did project a sense of wisdom. After all, he had navigated a treacherous system for many years and had risen to the position of headwaiter and unofficial president of all the staff. His word was law. Lamont grumbled a bit but took the knife from the table and walked upstairs to the kitchen very slowly. Then Mr. Washington—no one called him by his first name, not even the club's members—turned to Tom and said. 'Lamont's pretty bitter about things. He was a boxer, and a good one. The rumor is that he got hurt in a crooked fight. I don't know if the rumor is true or not. But Lamont goes crazy every once in a while. He's never hurt anyone. I guess he's all fuss and fuming. He'll leave you alone now. As long as you're down here, you're one of us. And everybody is equal at our table.'

"'When Tom returned to the patio, Albert took him aside. 'Don't worry about Lamont. He's all bark and no bite. Everybody's just glad you didn't call for the police and stood your ground.'

"'I was too scared to do anything else,' Tom admitted.

"'You've got no reason to be scared now. You can be accepted as one of us.'

"Tom knew that Albert was just trying to be nice, and he complimented Tom's work every chance he could just to make Tom feel better. Even Mr. Washington ventured out on the patio to congratulate Tom for doing a good job. Besides, Tom worked hard and the staff was short of busboys. So, Tom worked through to the end of his shift, around sunset when the patio closed.

"As he finished cleaning the last table, he caught sight of the girl who had jumped up on the bar, and Tom couldn't keep his eyes off her. Even when fully dressed in a white blouse and black clam diggers, her slender, alluring figure transfixed Tom. He didn't even notice the boy walking towards him.

"'Hey, isn't your name Tom? We met at the freshman orientation, remember.'

"'Sure, I remember." Actually Tom didn't, but thought he should fake it. He struggled to recall a name from that name-game they had played, but there were so many names and so many new faces. At last, a name sprung to his lips, 'Brandon, right.'

"'Yeah, that's right. I saw you staring at Holly. Who wouldn't stare? She's something else: rich, good lucking, You couldn't ask for much more. Holly is smart, too, sometimes too smart for her own good.'

"'Yeah, and she knows it, too, Brandon," Tom stated.

"'Yeah, well, she's my sister, just a year younger, so don't get any ideas. But look, on Mondays the club is closed. If you want you can come and use the pool.'

"All this while Albert was listening in.

"'No, thanks for the offer, but I don't think it would be right.'

"'Well, suit yourself. It's supposed to reach one hundred on Monday.'

"'Thanks for the offer, but I've got chores to do at home.'

"'All right, Tom. See you around.' Brandon left and headed to the white Lincoln waiting to take him home.

"Albert remarked simply, 'You did right, Tom.' Then returning to lock up the bar, he made a comment that stuck with Tom for the rest of his life. 'Hell, if I had jumped in the pool, they wouldda drained it, disinfected it, and repainted it, before they wouldda let any members plunge in.'

"When Tom got home, his mom asked him how his day went. He replied simply that he had learned a lot. That night, Tom couldn't keep himself from wondering why his American history classes had left out so much and how beautiful Holly was. He dreamed of what it would be like to have money for golf outings and eating out and never worrying about how to pay the bills. Maybe to have enough money to take Holly out.

"So, what do you think?" Phil asked.

Sly broke a momentary silence. "I'd say the kid was undergoing what they call a rite of passage. If he wouldda cried or something with that knife quivering in front of him, he wouldda failed. So, I guess the kid gets to move on."

"Humans just think they know everything," Amanda interjected. "They really know just what the history books and media tell them. But the ones who write those news releases and articles, and history books are just as flawed as the rest of the humans. Sometimes they don't even know that much more than the average guy on the street."

"Yeah, but you've got to give the humans some credit. I mean— with due apologies, Amanda— they don't go around sniffing butts," Pete commented.

"Naw, they just look for clues about social status. They ask stuff like what kind of car does the other guy drive, what neighborhood do they hang out in, where did they go to school, stuff like that. I don't know, maybe it's a better than sniffing butts." Sly was trying his best to keep Pete under control. Besides, he didn't want to lose his place as the resident smart aleck.

"Carrie, what do you think?" Phil asked.

"Thoughts of love and thoughts of death spring from the same seed," Carrie replied epigrammatically and enigmatically.

"Well, we'll see," Phil responded. "We have time for only two more episodes in this stage of Tom's life. So, here goes. The next morning, Tom took the early bus to work. He couldn't sleep and had turned over so many thoughts in his mind that the humdrum routine of the bus ride promised a welcome relief. He walked into work an hour early, fully expecting that he'd have to do no more than prepare the patio for the lunch crowd and maybe help to set tables in the main dining room. But the second day at work proved no less a challenge to his way of thinking than the first.

"'Tom, thank goodness you got here early. I'm serving a breakfast for the club's board of directors, and the rest of the waiters and busboys haven't come in yet. There's Mrs. Jones sitting out there on the deck. Approach her and ask her if there's anything she would like. I can tell you in advance what she'll order—a Bloody Mary. Then when she downs that one, wait no more than a minute and she'll order another one. Follow the same routine for two more times. Always ask politely and don't rush her. She'll end up sitting out there drinking until she's finished downing her daily breakfast of four Bloody Mary's." Tom could detect a certain urgency in the head waiter's words.

"'Excuse me, Mr. Washington, but I'm only fourteen. I don't think I can serve alcohol." Tom wasn't trying to get out of work or avoid an unpleasant encounter with the boozy Mrs. Jones. He just thought he was following the law.

"'Tom, you're all right. This is a private club and no one will complain. At least, I don't think you'll be taking sips from the drink the way the one waiter did. He got fired quick.'

"So, Tom followed Mr. Washington's instructions. Just as the headwaiter had forecast, Mrs. Jones was waiting expectedly for someone to take her order for the first of four drinks. She was sitting on the deck, nervously puffing away at a cigarette. Tom approached her and politely asked her if she would like anything. 'Yeah, Hon, bring me a Bloody Mary. The bartender will know how I like it—lots of Tabasco sauce with a stick of celery,' Mrs. Jones responded in a voice a bit hoarse from years of smoking.

"When Tom approached the bartender with the order, the middle aged man with a sagging paunch laughed a little and told Tom that he must be serving Mrs. Jones. 'I feel sorry for her even with all that money. All she does is try to wash down a lot of pain with a Bloody Mary. Let me know if you see her try to drive off, so I can call her oldest daughter who can come and get her. I don't want no drunk drivin' on my conscience. I just don't see why she doesn't divorce that SOB of a husband she's got.'

"Tom served Mrs. Jones her first of four drinks. He struggled a bit to appear pleasant and accommodating, but internally his mind was reeling. He had always thought that divorce was a problem, but in this instance maybe it was the solution. He didn't know. He was confused, dazed with new insights. As he bent down to take the silverware stored beneath the top of the patio bar, Albert walked up and grinned. 'I see you've met Mrs. Jones. She's a trip all right.'"

"You know what I think," Sly interjected. "I think Mrs. Jones shouldda gotten a job and then told that SOB of a husband to take a hike.' Sly seemed to mean what he had said as he pointed his right forepaw into the air to re-enforce his point.

"Pete said, 'Maybe the gal thought she was caught in a trap, sort of a steel trap of social expectations," Pete concluded.

Phil was taken aback by Pete's insight. Here he had thought that Pete's only concerns lay in eating and sleeping. "You know, a lot of people think that all we opossums do is to eat and sleep. And, yeah, we do a lot of that, but a lot of the time when it looks like we're only sleeping, we're just taking in the what's going on around us and trying to make sense of it all. But all of this thinking is hurting my head."

Carrie chimed in with her warning, "You've got five more minutes, Phil, for this session."

"Ok, I'll move it along, Phil replied. 'Tom worked all summer, made enough money for his books, and saved the rest of it, allowing himself only a few splurges at Dairy Queen. Every so often he'd steal a long look at Holly as she left the pool, wondering if she had even noticed him. Sooner than he had expected, Labor Day weekend was approaching and so was the end of his job. So, when Albert asked him if he would like to work a private party on the Saturday night of Labor Day Tom jumped at the chance to earn more money. Albert explained that this was no ordinary job. 'It'll mean lots of tips. Those guys will be playing poker all night and getting pretty plastered in the process. And, when they drink, they think they've got money runnin' out of their ass holes, so they tip like there's no tomorrow. We can make more in one night than we do in a whole week.'

"Albert was right. Tom found himself straining to keep up. The party of six started by slamming down the first round of drinks, four Scotch and sodas and two Tom Collins's. As soon as Tom cleared off the empty drinks and brought out more appetizers of cheese and sausage, they'd order another round. The six kept up this routine for two hours before two decided they had had enough for the night. They stopped playing poker but kept on drinking. One guy was getting desperate. He had already lost all of his money and he thought, if he had just one more chance to win it all back, he could still hold his head high. But after ten Scotch and sodas, his mind was lost in the miasma of a foggy blur. He had just bought a brand new 1965 model Ford Mustang, white with leather seats. He thought he had the winning hand, a full house of three aces and two eights—"

"That's even worse than a Dead Man's Hand," Carrie remarked.

"Yeah," Phil said. "The guy threw his car keys onto the table. 'See if you can match that!' he bellowed in a drunken swagger.

"'No problem,' the lone remaining player retorted. 'I'm calling your bluff.'

"Confident in his success, the Mustang owner spread out his cards on the table: three aces and two eights.

"'Not bad, not bad at all,' the rival said in a deadpan voice, 'but not good enough. Four kings.'

"The Mustang owner, or should I say former owners, bawled like a baby," Phil observed.

"Well, he should have," Amanda replied. "He was acting like one."

"You can't challenge Fate and win," Pete intoned.

"Sometimes, you just gotta know when to quit," Sly observed.

"Time's up," Carrie cawed.

"We'll meet again net week, same time, same place." Phil turned and strode away, all the while wondering why humans assumed they were the climax of evolution.

STAGE FIVE

ONGOING CHALLENGES

THE NEXT WEEK PHIL OPENED a new chapter in Tom's life. For the first time, all four of Phil's comrades assembled without any bickering or off-topic comments. Phil wasn't sure how to interpret this radical change in behavior, so he scanned the group, especially Sly, for any traces of temporarily suppressed mischievousness. He saw none. "Perhaps," Phil mused, "they're actually intent on our mission—or maybe they're just sleepy or maybe one or more of them is plotting some outburst or maybe they just want to get these sessions over with." In the meantime, he'd just have to continue.

"Whenever Tom gets nervous, he always wants to arrive early, so on the first day of school for freshmen, who had to start a day before the upperclassmen, Phil pestered his dad to get him to school early. 'I've got to be first in line to get the used books,' he explained. Tom's father deemed this a good reason to arrive early, so Tom got to school an hour ahead of time. He was sure that he would be the first one there. He wasn't. A dozen or more students were milling about, waiting for the bookstore to open, perhaps eager for their books, perhaps even more eager to get the bargain copies of used books."

"You know if I were in Tom's place, I probably would've slept in. I mean, really, how much money was he really going to save?" Pete protested. Phil exhaled. He knew that sooner or later one of the four would interrupt. He had figured on Sly, but Pete was also a likely candidate.

"That sounds just like you, Pete. I mean you're always lookin' for the easy way out. I get it. That Tom kid wants to save a few bucks. If you ask me, that's a sign good thinking." Sly stared at Pete as if his eyes were saying that Pete wasn't capable of any good thinking. Pete just ignored him.

"Well, I for one can understand why Tom was nervous. It's hard going somewhere new and not knowing anyone. Sometimes you've got to get into action just to get your mind off being so nervous and jittery." Amanda observed, with her head turned slightly to the right as if she were imagining Tom standing in line with his hands in his pants pockets, looking around at all of the strange, new faces.

Waiting until his colleagues were once again ready to listen, Phil continued, making a mental note of Amanda's empathy. "Tom did all of his books for English, algebra, and Latin for half price. But he had to purchase his physics and history textbooks new, carefully calculating how many hours of work it took to pay for each book. Once he bought his books, a senior volunteer took him and a group of other students on a tour, the first stop being the locker where they would store their books. Tom took out the padlock he had brought with him, tossed his books in the locker, and secured the padlock. Then to be sure, he opened it, using the combination he had memorized. He had a copy written down on a piece of paper that he kept in his wallet just in case. He watched as one student fumbled around with his padlock, getting redder and redder in the face all the time. Finally, the senior volunteer demonstrated how to open the lock. Tom would have gloated over this minor episode, but he knew he had practiced opening and closing his padlock for half an hour the night before. So, he was just relieved to have passed the first in a series of tests."

"You know, I'm getting' to like this Tom kid a little more. Maybe he's not such a bad guy, for a human I mean. He knows when to keep his mouth shut." Sly looked at his colleagues who didn't say a word. They didn't have to. Their facial expression said it all. The other four exhaled slightly and turned their heads aside and gazed up at empty space. Even Sly realized that they were evaluating him and not Tom. So, Sly meekly bowed his head and uttered a barely audible, "Sorry."

Phil returned to the book of Tom's life. "But the locker episode wasn't the only little test he had to pass. He had twenty minutes before he would run through his schedule of classes, so he stepped outside. Brandon exited a new Lincoln sedan. So did Holly. Brandon would be buying all new books, Tom figured, so he didn't have to hustle to get the bargains. Soon

Brandon—really Holly—was the center of attention, especially for the seven seniors who made a point of casually strolling over to greet the new freshman. Holly luxuriated in all of the attention as Brandon introduced her to the seniors, all of whom volunteered to help out Brandon in any way they could. 'So, Brandon, where does your sister go to school? I bet she'll be the prom queen somewhere.' Brandon casually dropped the fact that his younger sister was still in eighth grade, a fact that silenced the upperclassmen, who had no idea what to do next. Holly waved at the boys as she stepped back into the car and drove off while Brandon strolled over to the bookstore to pick up his books. As Tom watched, he knew he was entering a new world socially, a world whose unwritten rules and procedures would both entice and baffle him." Phil looked up and invited comments.

"I've known females like Holly. And I also know that sometimes things don't turn out for them all that well," Amanda observed.

"Yeah, you think maybe she'll end up like that four Bloody Mary lady at the country club?" Sly suggested. "What about it, Phil? You seem to have the lowdown on everybody."

"Not everybody, Sly. Just a select few and then I have to have authorization to discuss even them. As for Holly, we'll have to wait and see if she ever figures in Tom's life again."

Carrie cawed out, "Seventeen more minutes left."

"Then we'd better get on with our story," Phil determined. "Soon Tom found himself in his first class. The students sat alphabetically with their names taped to the assigned seat. It was an English class, so in the spare minutes before class started, the students milled about asking each other if they had done the summer reading, two novellas by John Steinbeck— *The Pearl* and *The Red Pony.* Tom had been assigned summer reading in his seventh and eighth grade year, so this was no surprise. The shock of recognition came when as far as Tom could tell all of the students except one had done the reading, and most had crammed it in the night before, so their knowledge was a little fuzzy. So, in his grade school days—days that seemed an eternity away—the teacher decided to just spend the first week of class having the students read what they were supposed to have read over the summer. Not this time. The teacher strode in just seconds before the bell to start class sounded. A second shock. The teacher was male. Previously all of Tom's teachers except for one, his fifth grade one, had been women. Tom had never given this reality a second thought. Only two of them were bad; the rest were good. They knew their material and explained it well. This teacher, Mr. Delacroix, a Jesuit scholastic, was about six feet tall, with a lean build and thinning black hair, which matched the black cassock he was wearing. He introduced himself and then passed out the test on the two Steinbeck novellas. At first, Tom and the rest of the students were frozen with the new reality. Most of them had anticipated an easy day: a boring lecture on the syllabus, some getting-to-know-you games, and that was about it. Even if they had a test, they thought, it would be no big deal, generic enough that they could ace it even if they had read only the Cliff's Notes. But not this one. It was short answer essay, ten questions in all, and the directions clearly stated that students had to back up their responses with evidence from the two stories. At first Tom wrote frenziedly. After a few minutes he paused to glance around and see how other students were doing. They, too, were immersed in a riot of writing—all but one who wrote calmly with a smirk on his face. 'He's probably just bullshitting,' Tom thought to himself. Later, when the teacher returned the graded tests the next day, Tom found out that he was right. The smirk was erased, and the kid hung his head low. Although this was the only test Tom had on that first day, all the teachers clearly meant business. Tom was competing against the best male students in the area, and he vowed he would succeed."

"Phil, is this how it's gonna be—a blow by blow description of each school day? I mean, come on, there's what, 180 school days a year, for four years! We're never gonna get through this." Sly objected.

Phil just grinned. "Why, Sly, I thought you wanted to make sure I wasn't keeping anything back. I offered you the chance to read all of the volumes on Tom as I have, but you decided against that."

"Yeah, well, that was then, and this is now."

"Don't worry, Sly. I'm giving you only the highlights and beginnings and ends tend to mark highlights. I'll adhere to the time limits for this session. We'll be done in, how long, Carrie?"

"Twelve minutes."

"Thanks, Carrie, that's twelve more minutes, Sly—twelve more minutes of on- task listening and assessing." Phil replied, stroking his chin,

"That is, if we have twelve more good minutes." Sly accepted his fate and silenced himself for the moment.

"All of his teachers focused on academics and students were expected to mirror this focus. Some did, but not all had the same relish for academic learning. A few who started the year left. There were daily quizzes in Latin and English and philosophy, weekly tests in algebra, history, and physics. Tom was so immersed in his studies that he had little time for anything else.

"But that changed a bit on the third Friday night of the school year."

"I'm glad to hear that," Pete chimed in. "I mean you know the saying all work and no play makes Jack—in this case, Tom—a dull boy. He needs to hang around a bit, have some fun."

"You're right, Pete." Phil responded. "And he was having fun. He joined in the cheers, saw upperclassmen paint themselves in the school colors, blue and white, and watched in awe as the varsity football team was rolling on to victory. There was only one disturbing thing—"

"He didn't have money to buy popcorn," Pete interrupted. Even Sly gave Pete a look of pure exasperation. Amanda shook her whole frame in disbelief while Carrie flapped her wings and momentarily took flight.

"No, Pete," Phil corrected him. "Holly walked by. It was still warm, so she was wearing white shorts cut low, so as much of her tanned complexion as she dared to expose was there for all to see. And see they did. Hundreds of eyes all focused on Brandon's eighth grade sister. Even a few of the scholastics couldn't restrain themselves from gawking a bit. Holly paraded around for what seemed like hours in front of Tom's mind. Actually, she was up from her seat for only the brief few minutes it took to buy a Coke, but sometimes time must be measured psychologically and not chronometrically. All that night, she stood in Tom's mind."

"Who won the game?" Sly asked.

Amanda snapped a reply, "Holly was the clear winner."

Phil surveyed his small audience, noting that Amanda had had the last word. "Time to move on," Phil remarked. "For the next year and a half, Tom immersed himself in his studies. He'd go to class, go home, study and go to bed. He still worked occasional weekend jobs at the country club; he still put in his forty-four hours a week at he same club during the summer. He still dreamed of Holly almost every night. Otherwise, his life was cruising along. His younger brother Pete followed his path, and his even younger sister Grace continued the family tradition. All was going smoothly—except for one factor: geometry class. Tom admired the scholarly bent of almost all of his teachers. Only one of these defied expectations or, perhaps, just didn't suit Tom. Mr. Groberkopf was only in his early thirties, but he looked and acted as if he were in his doddering eighties. He attached himself to the podium in the front of the class and never left it. He never explained any of the concepts unless a student asked a very specific question. Since some knowledge is necessary to ask intelligent, specific questions, at first no one ever asked any questions. A few of the better students in math—Tom was not among them—did start to ask questions, but Tom suspected that their parents were really the ones who had come up with the questions. Tom toiled away at geometry but felt as if he were cast aside in stormy waters on a sinking ship. Finally, whether by luck, perseverance, or insight, the mysteries of geometry began to evolve into problems that even Tom's adolescent reasoning could fathom. He survived geometry.

"But more pressing issues troubled young Tom. Paradoxically, the less Tom had seen Holly, the more strongly he yearned for her."

"Yeah, you know, that's the way it is. The more you can't have something, the more you want it. Take me, for instance. One time, somebody dropped a half-drunk bottle of Natural Light beer. So, of course, me being who I am, gulped down the contents. It was good, but the eight ounces I imbibed were too much for a twenty pound body. So, I got sick and resolved never to drink again. I didn't. Besides who leaves half-full bottles of beer around? I mean, other than some kid who was sneaking a drink and didn't want to get caught. Still, for months I could taste that cold beer going down my gullet and I savored every minute of it. You just want what you can't have." So concluded Sly.

Amanda joined in. "Boys get in trouble when they do one of two things: imagine that girls are angelic perfections or that they are demonic whores."

Pete suggested that Tom would feel a lot better if he got more sleep instead of dreaming of a girl he barely knew.

Carrie commented briefly, "Time's running out."

"Carrie's right," Phil acknowledged. The other issue that troubled

Tom was the real presence of Christ in the Eucharist. He felt so unworthy, especially on the day of the junior retreat when the retreat master spoke from the pulpit, his accusing face illuminated by the only light in the otherwise darkened chapel. He warned the boys of the sin of masturbation. He claimed that the army had special exercises that would identify those who masturbated. He warned them of the fires of hell and begged them to ask for forgiveness and to sin no more. Like the other boys there, Tom felt horribly guilty and unworthy, so unworthy that he wondered whether or not he should ever again receive Communion even after he had confessed his sin. With his doubts and guilt tormenting him, Tom volunteered for every sodality mission to help the poor. He tried to pray even more ardently. He loaded and unloaded tray after tray of food to aid the poor. He was considered the exemplar of the sodality spirit. Only Tom knew that his feverish prayer and acts of mercy kept him in a fog of activity that kept him from seeing his doubts and misgivings."

Carrie cawed out. "Only a few more minutes, Phil."

"Yeah, let's wind things up," Sly seconded.

"In his senior year," Phil continued. "Many of Tom's troubles found at least a temporary relief."

"He went out with Holly," Pete yelled out.

"No, Pete, the answer came in English Lit class." Phil countered.

"You've got to be kiddin' me, right, Phil?"

"No, I'm not, Pete. Tom and his classmates were studying Chaucer's *Canterbury Tales.*"

"Hey, that can be a little risqué at times, right." Sly interrupted.

"Yes, it can, but it also addresses some serious issues. Some never get past the risqué tales," Phil noted, looking directly at Sly. "The teacher, a balding middle-aged man who had the habit of reaching out his right arm and scratching his forehead, explained the background of Courtly Love. While he lectured, more than a few students were noting down very carefully how may times he scratched his head. But Tom found the entire discussion personally relevant. The first component of Courtly Love was love at first sight. 'Well,' Tom thought, 'that certainly fits me. I 've never even spoken with Holly, but I can't get her out of my mind.' The second perquisite of CL, the teacher droned on, was that this love at first sight took place in a garden or church. Tom reasoned that a country club swimming pool was close enough to the modern version of a medieval garden (maybe even a church). The third characteristic was that the beloved was unattainable either because she was already married or she had taken a vow of virginity or, like Juliet, she descended from a rival faction or enemy. Tom pondered this trait for a while.' We don't have aristocrats and serfs any more, but we do have the rich, the super rich, the middle class, and the poor working class. I think the class barrier can count in this case. The senior prom was coming up, and Tom had briefly flirted with the idea of asking Holly, but the senior class president had already asked her and she had accepted. 'Besides,' Tom consoled himself, 'not only have I not spoken to Holly, but I hadn't even exchanged more than a dozen words with her brother Brandon in the four years of high school.' Then, as the instructor elaborated, the frustrated lover writes sonnets or other poetry to express his deep frustration and loss. 'I haven't written any sonnets—that's true—but I have thrown all of my energies into my studies, in some sort of sublimation, I guess.'

"So, Tom found some comfort in realizing that he was not alone in his dilemma. He went on to do all of the usual high school activities. He ran cross country and track but set no records. He went to the Senior Prom with a girl a friend had set him up with. She was nice enough, Tom thought, but no Holly."

Amanda couldn't contain herself. "That Tom is as foolish as ever. He should at least have taken the time to get to know the girl he escorted to the prom. He might have found out that she had a lot more to offer than that Miss Holly."

"You're right," Phil agreed. "But Tom was still young and dumb, just as most of us were during our adolescence. But there was still another troubling dilemma for Tom. He felt so conflicted about receiving Communion both because of his own doubts and because of his own feelings of guilt and inadequacy."

"So, what did the kid do?" Sly wanted to know.

"He talked with the teacher who had lectured on Courtly Love. Tom instinctively felt that romance and religion were somehow interconnected. When Tom explained his misgivings about receiving Communion, the teacher, who was also a Jesuit priest, listened intently and then spoke. 'I don't have all of the answers, Tom. But I do know this. It's good that you have doubts. That means you're taking the issue seriously and not just casually accepting the sacraments without an ounce of thought. None of us are worthy of Communion. If we were, we wouldn't need it. We're all weak and fallible in so many different ways. Go to Communion because you are weak and need all the help God will provide for you. We have the sacraments not because we are perfect. We receive them because we are so imperfect.'

"Tom took in all that he had heard. He still had his doubts. He still would have to work out the issues he was facing, but doing so would take a lifetime."

"So, that's it for now?" Sly implored.

Carrie glanced at her watch and pronounced, "Time's up for today."

STAGE SIX

COLLEGIATE WINS AND LOSSES

"H OO, BOY," SLY EXCLAIMED AS he made his way to the Convocation Area. "Now we're getting to the good stuff: beer bongs, frat parties, guys and gals in togas making like Caligula, retching all over the place. Let the good times roll, man." He sat down on his haunches and rubbed his forepaws together in gleeful anticipation. "Finally some action!"

Amanda then stepped in, overheard Sly talking to himself and asked, "Sly, what are you talking about?"

"Hey, pretty lady, it's college and the sixties, you know, wild parties, drunken orgies, the pungent aroma of pot raining down like a tropical storm, protests, sit-ins, the Beatles, the Stones, the stoned, and the wild, free sex, mini-skirts, long hairs, and wild times at Woodstock, all that sixties stuff, Miss Priss."

"Sly, you weren't even alive then. How do you know all of this?" Amanda snorted back.

"Hey, me and Pete—you see him scurryin' in—we watch Animal House every chance we get. Hey, sometimes we even take a gander at the History Channel. That's we found out about Woodstock. Man, those were the days!"

"They weren't all wild and good," observed Phil as he slowly made his way. Carrie followed him, swooping down from above. "There were assassinations—Jackie Kennedy, Dr. Martin Luther King, Jr, Robert Kennedy. There were boys maybe a year out of high school slogging their way through the jungles of Viet Nam in a war that no one understood. There were sit-ins and protests, all right, and there were beatings and upheavals. People spat on each other. Americans broke into factions. No, it wasn't all fun and games—at least for most people it was an era of tough times and even tougher decisions."

"So, we're not gonna hear about Tom sowin' his wild oats and partyin' hardy and all that good kind of stuff?" Sly almost whined as the words slid out of his mouth.

"No, my friend," Phil remarked in an even voice. "The times, they were, indeed, a-changin' in some ways for the good, in other ways for the bad, and in most cases, just changin', neither good nor bad, just different."

"Let's hear a little about the good first before we have to deal with the bad," Amanda requested.

"Agreed?" Phil looked around, and finding no dissent started up. "Carrie, would you start the clock for this session?"

"Of course, although I still find it odd to be discussing time when we live in eternity. I guess we can live in both worlds, the one of the lasting now and the one of change and flux."

Momentarily taken back by Carrie's uncharacteristic reflection, Phil paused a bit before continuing his story. "Ok, first the good. Tom still worked at the country club, graduating from busboy to waiter in the process. And in the summer of Tom's senior year, one major change shook the whole serenity of the gently rolling hills and quiet rounds of golf and formal dinners at the country club."

"I know, I know," Sly blurted out. "Tom got Holly pregnant." Amanda at first shook her head and then shook her whole body as if she were trying to rid herself of some troublesome pest.

"No, Sly, Tom never went out with Holly. She remained the girl of his dreams, maybe even, what happened at the country club heralded a new era."

"Oh, come on, Phil," Pete objected. You sound like you're just a mediocre journalist when you say that. I should know. I sleep in piles and piles of tossed out newspapers. They keep me warm. When I get bored, I even read some of them, so I can get sleepy again."

"Point well taken, Pete," Phil acknowledged. I guess it's easy to get swept away in a current of clichés."

"Phil, you're at it again. Just keep it plain and simple." Pete looked around for approval. All were nodding their heads in agreement, even Phil.

"Ok, here it goes, plain and simple. The country club had hired a black manager. Except for Tom and later his younger brother Peter, all of the servers, cook, and busboys had been black, even one or two of the head cooks. The club never gave them the title of chef, but they really were. But now, the country club had named a black manager. He seemed all right to Tom, especially after the chief administrator complimented Tom on his work. Less than a handful of members complained. One disgruntled member approached Tom, trying to win him over. 'Hey, Tom, you know that new manager?" Tom responded that he had met him. 'Well, what do you think of working for a black man?' The man sounded accusatory. Tom hesitated a bit because he had to choose his words carefully and not offend a member, even a racist one. Tom said that he was pleased to work for whomever the club chose. The member didn't get the answer he had hoped for, but he really couldn't accuse Tom of anything. So, the guy just mumbled on and on and left.

"Tom would see his boss soon again but in a very different environment. His university was sponsoring a Black Awareness day, and Tom thought he could go and check it out after his last class. The great hall in the student union center had been transformed to resemble a West African village on its north side. In the village, goldsmiths, or at least actors playing the role of goldsmiths, provided demonstrations of their trade. Other tradesmen and artisans also displayed their work. The south side of the great hall featured famous African-Americans like Frederick Douglas, Sojourner Truth, Medgar Evers, Ruby Bridges, Langston Hughes, Zora Neale Hurston, and many others. The display honoring Dr. Martin Luther King, Jr, occupied the center of the wall and served as a focal point. Docents stood at the tables and answered questions about each of the figures. Breakout rooms allowed small groups to discuss specific figures and moments in African-American culture such as one for jazz and blues, another for literature, another for dancers and artists and photographers. One room was devoted to African-American oral culture and folklore. Tom wandered about, one of only a few white people present. At the breakout room featuring black entrepreneurs, Tom saw Mr. Bledsoe, the newly appointed manager of the country club where Tom worked. Across the room the two exchanged a brief wave, and then Tom knew he was out of place. It wasn't Mr. Bledsoe's reaction that befuddled him. After all, he was only a part-time waiter. One bystander who witnessed the brief exchange between Tom and his boss, whispered 'What the hell is that white kid doing here?' Suddenly Tom felt he was out-of-place and left out. He had had a brief taste of what it feels like to be excluded. Everyone else at the Awareness Day acted friendly. A few even mentioned that they were glad that white people had stopped by even if only a handful had managed to do so. Perhaps Tom over-reacted or perhaps hadn't yet learned to shrug some criticism off and just do what you think is right. Still, he suddenly just wanted to leave. He wondered if he had intruded upon a private moment when black Americans were studying their roots and accomplishments, if, perhaps, he was viewed as a foreign, hostile white presence. On the other hand, he found the exhibits informative. He wondered what his boss at the country club felt.

"It wouldn't be the only time that Tom felt alone and ostracized. While people were marching in their streets for racial justice, many young men were marching off to war in distant Viet Nam. As a boy growing up, Tom had envisioned himself as the heroic figure, defending our country and, perhaps, dying a martyr's death in defense of democracy. He had immersed himself in the Hollywood version of war while his father looked on, shaking his head and wondering when his son would face the grim realities. Some of Tom's grade school friends had been drafted less than a year out of high school graduation. Tom felt ashamed of his college deferment, so he did the next best thing. He enrolled in the Army ROTC program at his school. At first he felt proud, learning some of the basics of military life: chain of command, the history of the US military, basic organizational structure, and many other matters. Some aspects of the military Tom found mildly annoying. He didn't understand the stress on marching. 'It's not as if soldiers are fighting in such large, massed formations any more,' he thought as he went through one marching drill after another. 'Machine guns and modern artillery have made that kind of fighting obsolete.' Still, he felt a certain pride in the exercises. Yet on those days when he had to wear his uniform on campus, his mere presence generated hostile stares and whispered comments as people turned aside and did everything they could to condemn him privately. But soon private condemnation yielded to public outcry. One morning, at the same time as the Tet offensive was going on in remote Viet Nam, he heard cries of 'Baby killer' and 'When the Revolution comes, you'll be the first to go.'

Tom just plodded on, pretending not to hear. The captain in charge of the ROTC unit observed that militarily the Tet offensive had failed. However, politically, it succeeded. The unit commander ordered the cadets not to wear their uniforms in public. But that command made no difference. Their neatly trimmed haircuts gave the cadets away.

"So Tom did what he had always done," Phil commented.

"He joined a commune and had riotous group sex," a bored Sly interjected.

"Sly, if say something at least let it make some sense. Otherwise, don't interrupt." Amanda snapped.

"Yeah, I don't see this Tom guy doing anything other than falling in love with the first bimbo he meets. When do we get to the romance part?" Pete asked.

"In due time, Pete," Phil explained. "Carrie, add on another minute to the time for today's session, thanks to Sly's off-topic nonsense."

"It wasn't off topic at all," Sly objected. I heard about the sexy sixties, so I know what was going on." Sly was doing his best to shift the blame for the added time.

"But you don't know what was going on in Tom's case. You also don't know what was going on in the minds of those guys who were fighting in a war that didn't garner any popular support. They fought for a variety of reasons. Most were drafted and accepted their fate. After all, the draft had been around from World War II on. Many of their fathers had been drafted, so they were just following the law and family tradition. Others fought because they absolutely believed they were doing their patriotic duty to defeat Communism. They had heard of Khrushchev's threat, 'We will bury you,' and took the threat seriously. Perhaps a few viewed war as an opportunity to escape harsher realities at home. An even smaller few thought of war as an opportunity to get ahead and cash in."

"Ok, Phil, I get it, we can't judge people's motives because we don't know what they were. And the 'baby killer' stuff is BS. Still, what about the frat parties and wild stuff that was going on?"

Here Amanda took over and asked a pointed question, "Just how many people were doing the crazy stuff?"

"I don't know for sure," Phil commented, a bit relieved that the conversation had taken a turn towards reason. "But many students were just like Tom, studying and working part-time to prepare for a better life or at least one in which they didn't have to scrounge around at the end of the month for money. I don't know the exact percentage of those regarded as the 'Flower Children' and those who weren't. But I suspect that the majority weren't really hippies but ones who did wear psychedelic clothes, maybe smoked some joints and took a few other illegal drugs, wore bellbottom jeans, and sported funky haircuts—all of these things from time to time. Tom had even overheard his captain talking to some Air Force pilots in the administrative office of the ROTC building. These pilots flew bombers and fighters but thought the war was unwinnable. 'It just doesn't make sense,' one pilot commented, 'to risk a six million dollar aircraft to blow up a fifty dollar bridge that will just be rebuilt the next day.' Even Tom's commanding officer chimed in. 'Yeah, we're winning the body count, but so what? We're not nation building. We're just nation destroying. I just don't think that most of the people we're fighting are out to bury us. They just want better lives for their children—just as we do.' Tom was shaken. He had learned that the motto of the Air Force Strategic Air Command was 'Peace is our Profession, —strength through overwhelming military power.' Now he was wondering if force alone could ever effect any permanent peace. Maybe those boyhood dreams of glory were only sad delusions?

"Tom's doubts were reinforced from a second source. Do you remember when I said that Tom did what he always had done?"

"Yeah, Phil, I remember," Sly said dryly. I tried to answer that and got in trouble."

"For good reason, Sly," Amanda added."

"Yeah, so what did Tom usually do?" a disgruntled Sly asked.

"He drowned his doubts in study, retreated to a world of books so he didn't have to interact with a world he didn't understand." Phil answered. His studying did have one good practical result. He won scholarships, but it also isolated him. However, in Tom's Philosophy of Man course, the professor argued that in the nuclear age, in which world annihilation loomed as a very real option, war was obsolete. 'The imminent possibility of total world annihilation makes everyone the loser. In previous wars, some would win the spoils of war and some would lose, but the possibility of winning always tempted the warmongers. No more.'"

"Yeah, Pete and I watched that movie, *Dr. Strangelove or How I stopped Worrying and Loved the Bomb.* At least I think that was the name of it. Pete and I got a real kick out of the part where the cowboy / pilot rides the nuclear bomb down to its target, just hollerin' 'Yee-ha, Yee-ha' and waving his cowboy hat like it was some kind of rodeo or somethin'. Anyways people were all hyped up about the world getting' blown to pieces and everything. I think the film came out around Tom's time."

Amanda had busied herself on her cell phone, checking out the movie. "Right, Sly, it came out in 1964, so Tom probably would have known about it even if had hadn't seen it.'

"So," Phil continued, "Tom felt alone and isolated again. He was becoming disillusioned with his whole childhood dreams of military glory but didn't feel any kinship with the ones who had cried 'Babykiller' at him either."

"So what did he do?" Pete asked. "Just hang around on a tree."

"Metaphorically, yes, only he just hung around in a library carrel, alone and isolated. He quit the ROTC program and then belonged to nothing. Instead of playing on a soccer team, he took long runs on his own but never competed."

Amanda reflected. "Being alone all the time can be dangerous. Humans and canines are pack animals after all."

"You're right, Amanda," Phil agreed.

"Yeah, yeah, yeah, Amanda's always right in Phil's mind," Sly grumbled.

Phil chose to ignore Sly's grousing and continued "Being off on one's own island creates all types of delusions and distortions. Tom was in his early twenties, a time when the sexual urges sometimes get mixed up with all types of other ideas."

"Now we're getting' to it," Sly whispered to Pete, rubbing his forepaws together in anticipation of something erotic, relishing the thought of voyeuristic exploration of Tom's anticipated sordid sexual adventures.

Phil paused to allow Sly's fantasies settle down. "Don't get too excited, Sly. What I'm going to tell you may be disappointing. Alone in his library carrel, Tom idealized his lust and formulated a life far removed from the world where 'ignorant armies clashed by night.' In this fantasy island, Tom would live atop a craggy cliff on an isolated peninsula with only his bride."

"This Tom guy has gone wacko," Pete said. "I mean where is he gonna get food on this lonely outcropping? He doesn't know how to grow it and, even if he manages to grow it, he probably couldn't keep the likes of Sly or me from stealing it. This guy has a lot of growing up to do. You know there's no fool like a young fool, to add a new twist to an old saying."

"Well, Pete, even Tom realized that he was indulging in fantasy. Sometimes he envisioned himself as Rick, the expatriate American, in *Casablanca*, heroically rejecting his lady-love for a noble cause."

Sly added, "Ok, I get it. This is sorta like that Medieval Courtly Love stuff. You know two lovers torn apart by forces they can't control, the long-suffering lover, and that part about the Paris experience. That was sorta like love at first sight, right. And then the Rick guy marches off at the end to fight the forces of evil, the Nazis. That storyline ties up romance and military glory all in one. Only Tom doesn't have any Nazis to shoot."

"You're right, Sly. There wasn't any convenient enemy to chase. Tom found himself caught. He thought the Viet Nam War was just a futile exercise in piling up the body count but a lot of the loudest protestors didn't appeal to him at all. They'd yell 'Baby-killer' at guys who sincerely believed they were sacrificing their comfortable lives stateside for a noble cause. It seemed in that crazy era that the ones who thought they were the most right were doing the most harm. That's why Tom retreated to his books, that's why he yearned for a romantic escape. He had forgotten just one important factor." Phil surveyed his four comrades, waiting for a response.

Finally, Carrie broke the silence. "So, what did Tom forget?" she asked before cawing out, "Only a few minutes left in this session."

"Yeah," Sly seconded. "Get to the point, Phil."

"He forgot that he wasn't any better or any worse than 99.9 % of the people around him. All that studying was paying off. Tom was earning straight *A*'s and won academic awards in English, Latin, and history. But the high grades and awards blinded him to his own faults. He felt secure in his success. He deluded himself into thinking that he was too smart to make any mistakes. At an awards ceremony just a week before graduation, Tom sat in the first row and beamed as the dean of Arts & Sciences called for him to stand up and receive his honors, not once but five times: Phi Beta Kappa, the Intercollegiate Latin prize, Dean's list for four years, class valedictorian, winner of a full tuition scholarship to graduate school. As he stood to receive the awards that came showering down on him, he grew more and more assured of his own success. He thought he could do no wrong. He had been seeing a young woman for three months and that's when he proposed. He felt they were soul mates, but—"

"They weren't. Tom got blinded by the bright lights of his own minor successes," Amanda commented. "This looks like a sure formula for disaster: young man with romantic delusions + naïve assumptions of continued success = future disaster and disillusionment."

"Yep," Phil concurred. "Tom's younger brother Pete tried to warn him about his hasty engagement. And Pete was only a sophomore in high school at the time. Even his younger sister Grace, only in eighth grade, didn't like her future sister-in-law. 'I think they're both idiots,' she concluded."

"But there's no fool like a young fool," Sly grinned as he echoed the sentiments of his buddy Pete. "I just hope that this Tom guy begins to wise up."

"Time's up," Carrie cawed as she took flight and swept over them.

STAGE SEVEN

LIFE BEYOND GRADUATION

"ALL RIGHT, PHIL, SO YOU'RE calling us together so we can wrap this whole thing up. Tom-boy and his beautiful wife live happily ever after. Tom becomes a multi-millionaire, is thronged by admiring crowds, blah, blah, blah." Sly was irritated that his wild rumpus through the trashcans of eternity had been interrupted by this weekly duty.

"You've got it all wrong, Sly," an exasperated Phil replied in a slow, measured voice. "The story is just beginning."

"I was afraid of that," a chastened Sly muttered.

"I'd like to know what did Tom's parents think of his engagement to a girl he barely knew," Amanda asked.

"Good question," Phil answered.

Mumbling away and curled up in a ball to further muffle his voice, Sly whispered to Pete. "Oh, yeah, Amanda's always got the right question. It's Amanda this, Amanda that. That canine spent way too much time around humans."

Pete whispered back to Sly, keeping one eye fixed on Phil, whom he didn't want to antagonize. "You know, Sly, Amanda's got a point. Young bucks who get a taste of a little success think they know it all and rule over all. The guy's gonna be heading for a downer, a fall from the top branches to the frozen ground below. You know the old saying 'Pride goes before the fall.'"

"Pete, so when did you start becoming a philosopher?" Sly wanted to know.

"I've been thinkin' all week long. Phil wouldn't be callin' us together unless there was a problem. This Tom kid thinks he knows everything; he's had some minor successes, and some minor failures that he doesn't think about. He's got one eye closed. I don't know. I think maybe the story really is just starting."

Phil had allowed them to continue their little tete-a-tete as he sensed just as Tom's arrogance masked a deep feeling of inadequacy, so, too, did Sly's. "You know, Amanda's got a question. Tom's younger brother Pete thought his older brother must have been dropping acid or something. Why would he hook up with some girl now, he wondered. The Viet Nam war was winding down; there was talk of the draft ending. His older brother could just focus on grad school. "Tom always told me to concentrate on school and get good grades, and let loose some energy by playing soccer. Why can't he do the same and follow his own advice?" In eighth grade, Tom's younger sister Grace summed it all up: "The two of them think they're Romeo and Juliet, but I guess they forget how that story ended."

Here Amanda burst out, "But what about Tom's parents? Surely he would listen at least a little to them."

"You forget, Amanda, that this was the Flower Generation. They were going to transform the world they inherited from their parents' generation into the Age Of Aquarius: make love, not war, harmony throughout the world, and transcendental bliss."

"Yeah, well, we don't even have that here in the afterlife," Sly observed. "Now don't get me wrong. We've got it really good here, and I wouldn't want to be anywhere else, but you know how it goes. We still have our little squalls and tiffs."

"Yes, Sly, we're well aware of that. Thanks for reminding us." Phil let loose with a sigh of exasperation. "You see, Tom wasn't the only one who had bought into that Courtly Love stuff. His parents ardently believed that Fate had drawn two lovers together and that love really could occur at first sight. So, they reluctantly went along with the wedding plans even though Tom had little money and perhaps even less common sense."

"Hey, Sly, I don't think you have to worry about that happily-ever-after stuff," Pete shouted out. "I was beginning to wonder when some practical realities would enter the picture. That Tom kid had it pretty good, thanks to his parents. Now he had to start acting on his own, learning from mistakes. And it looks as if he's going to make a lot of them."

"Good insight, Pete," Phil remarked. "Within six months, Tom and his bride started arguing about money—mainly that there wasn't enough of it. The trouble began on the trip east as Tom and his bride were heading to his graduate school. Tom had bought an inexpensive VW Bug with a reconditioned engine. Of course, back then, a lot of people were driving VW Bugs—great for city driving but on long hauls on the interstates, well that's a different story. The first six hours of the trip went well enough maybe because of the novelty of it all. But on a stop for gas, the troubles began. Tom turned the ignition key on—Nothing. It was hot, real hot as the temperature soared close to 100.

"'Lexie, the car won't start,' Tom explained as she strolled out of the gas station with a cool iced tea in hand."

"'What do you mean, it won't start? It was cruisin' along just fine before we stopped.'"

"'Yeah, well, it won't start now,' an annoyed Tom replied."

"An old, white haired and white bearded trucker sauntered over. "Sorry, folks, I couldn't help but overhearing. It seems to me that that VW has got vapor lock. A lot of them air-cooled engines can't handle the heat. I'm sorry to that there's not much to be done other than just wait it out until the engine cools down. You might want to plan on doin' your drivin' at night when it's not so damn hot.'"

"Tom thanked the man and just stared at the immoveable object. "You're not doing any good just standin' there gawking at it, Tom' Lexie complained. 'I don't know about you, but I'm getting in the air conditioned gas station and drink my iced tea. For all I care, you can stand out here sweatin' in the heat. This never would have happened if you hadn't bought that cheap car.'"

"Tom didn't say much. He thought he couldn't complain much because there was some truth in what Lexie was saying. He thought he could save some money so they'd have enough for the apartment he had rented. He was praying that that wasn't a mistake, too. The university rented out apartments for married grad students, so Tom had put his faith in that."

"I'll bet he was wrong," Pete blurted out. You see, we opossums always check out the tree or culvert where we'll be hangin' out first. And we always make sure to eat as much as we can so we've got lots of fat to store up for lean times. Tom hadn't done either one of those things."

Sly was thinking, 'That's not the only reason you're so fat.' But, for once, he kept that comment to himself.

"After three hours of inventing excuses for staying in the gas station so long, enduring the harsh glares of the cashier who suspected that something questionable was going on—you know, like the couple was some kind of Bonnie and Clyde duo just waiting for the right moment to strike—Tom went out and tried to start the car. This time it started up. Without saying a word, Lexie huffed her way out to the car, got in, and just pursed her lips. They were on their way. Tom drove for two hours and then waited for the sun to go down and cool things off before he started up again for the last four-hour leg of his trip."

Amanda observed that maybe it was a good sign that Tom was following the old trucker's advice. Sly and Pete concurred. Carrie just had cartoon-like visions of the vultures circling overhead while two wayfarers crawled along the desert sand under the glaring eye of a hostile sun.

"It was midnight when the couple pulled into the parking space reserved for their apartment. The apartments were furnished, so Tom had to haul in only their suitcases of clothes. Still, the two were worn out and just plopped down on the bed. The next morning they awoke and took a look out the window. There was trash everywhere: beer cans, discarded pizza boxes, cartons for Chinese take-out, some broken vodka bottles, and a few rats scurrying about. Tom recalled that the scene bore no resemblance to the pictures he had seen on the brochure. Lexie screamed out, 'What kind of hell-hole have you taken me to? This isn't what you had told me.' Tom meekly replied that the scene before them didn't look at all like the photos he had seen. 'You idiot, of course, they don't. You can't believe everything you see on ads.' Lexie stormed out, 'I'm going somewhere where the rats don't live.' She came back two hours later while Tom wondered what kind of mess he had gotten himself into. She came back, reeking with the pungent smell of pot smoke still clinging to her hair and blouse. Tom didn't say a word as he busied himself cleaning out the area in front of their apartment and even the spaces in the two adjoining apartments. The manager made his way over to Tom and asked him if he were applying for the custodian job. Tom, said he wasn't, that he just couldn't stand the filth. The manager casually turned his back and just let out a casual 'Whatever,' and made his way back to the office.

"In the three days before classes started, Tom bought his books and acquainted himself with the campus and spent some time touring the library, where he figured he'd spend most of his time. Lexie busied herself applying for jobs. 'After all,' she reasoned, 'pot isn't cheap.' She got a job as the receptionist for a small legal office in the downtown area of the university. She felt that it wouldn't hurt to have a few lawyers on her side."

"Oh, yeah, I can see what's comin' now,' Sly burst out. "It's gonna be either divorce or a pot rap. I can see it comin' and Tommy-boy wasn't one the wiser, I'll bet."

"You've got good reasons for your suspicions, Sly, at least for some of them. Tom was too worried about doing well in his grad courses. In fact, he was so absorbed in his own worries that he really wasn't thinking about Lexie and their relationship. He just assumed that things would work their way out. He knew that his parents had sometimes argued—but not for very long. And in the end, things turned out Ok. He assumed the same would happen with Lexie and him."

"Yeah, but you know what the first three letters of *assume* are, don'tcha" Sly grinned. "Yeah, I can look around and see. You got it: ass, and right now Tommy-boy is an ass through and through."

"Maybe you shouldn't judge Tom so harshly, Sly. Sometimes the same could be said of you." Amanda declared what Phil had been thinking."

Sly countered with, "Yeah, but I'm no Tommy-boy."

"Perhaps not or perhaps so," Phil said. "But let's go on with the story. Tom's first class shattered any delusions he may have had about succeeding only because of hard work and determination. Tom had arrived early and taken a seat. He always came early when he felt nervous or unsure, and on the first day of classes almost everyone felt nervous and unsure. The professor, Dr. Oldcastle, arrived promptly at the start of class. set a few books down, sat down at the desk, and began poring over some documents. Based upon reputation alone, the instructor was so formidable that no mere student would ever presume to challenge him. He had earned the right to an endowed chair, he had written multiple scholarly articles and several books on Victorian poetry. He had also acquired the reputation as the gatekeeper for graduate students. Those who succeeded in winning his approval went on for jobs in prestigious institutions. Those who didn't—well, no one knew whatever became of them. At age fifty-nine, the professor had reached the height of his career. He was tall, approximately six feet, two inches with a lean build. He sported a grey, tweed suit despite the warm weather, a white shirt and a multi-colored bow tie. His wire rim glasses grew to sinister size as he read over the class roster. 'I see we have a number of students here who attended a glut of saint universities: St. Bonaventure, St. Louis, St. Mary's, etc. etc. etc. It also appears that a number of students here have Irish surnames.' Here Tom shuddered a bit, for he did, indeed, have an Irish last name. He pursed out his lips ever so slightly in apparent disgust. Professor Oldcastle, Tom later learned, was a notorious Anglophile, and it had been only eight months since Bloody Sunday or the Bogside Massacre, and the Northern Irish Troubles were only starting. Tom hadn't reflected much on his Irish heritage, as he was two generations removed from it. Oh, he and his family celebrated St. Patrick's Day. He recalled that his mother would chant,' Potatoes and fishes make mighty fine dishes on Patty's Day in the morning.' His family attended and sometimes marched in the St. Patrick's Day parade. Last March, Tom did recall the bitterness in his father's voice when his dad lashed out: 'Twenty-six people shot by the Brits and for doing what? Protesting against internment without trial. Putting people away in prisons and camps for as long as they pleased. No good will come of this.' His father was right. The violence—the car bombings, the midnight assassinations—had only just begun. Inwardly, Tom wondered if he would be the victim of a conflict thousands of miles away."

"So, did the professor give Tom the ax?" Sly asked. "I mean the kid has had it pretty good until now, so good that he just don't know how the world works."

"Sly, the whole reason the humans get into so much trouble is because they get a stupid mindset and then let that mindset, that bias, get in the way of their thinking. Sometimes canines act the same way. Just because I'm a poodle, some other dogs assume I'm all prim and proper."

"Well, Amanda, you are," Sly retorted.

"Maybe so, but I've got loud bark and a hard bit and shredding claws when I want to." Amanda was growling.

"Ok, Ok, I get it, Amanda," Sly said, backing off from the tight circle.

Phil tried to rein in the brewing discontent. "Let's get back to our mission. We've got time, don't we, Carrie?"

"Plenty of time. Do you want me to add more?"

"That won't be necessary, will it?" Phil looked around at the now contrite Sly and chastened Amanda. They both responded in unison, "No, we're ready to get back to our work."

"Good," Phil belted out. "Let's get to it. Well, Tom just repressed the memory of that first day of class until midway through the term. He got a message that he was summoned to Professor Oldcastle's office. He knew this wasn't good. He wasn't the best student in the class, but he was far from the worst. Ten students had already withdrawn from the class. Tom thought that maybe he should join them. He loathed Professor Oldcastle, but he knew he was finished with grad school if he didn't at least make a *B* in the course. Still reeling a bit from the rancor—his own and Professor Oldcastle's—of that first day of class, Tom realized that he hadn't been giving his best efforts in the class. Instead, he had thrown himself into excelling in his other classes—Renaissance drama, Chaucer, and Old English literature. He was doing well in all of those. As he understood, he ranked right in the middle of Professor Oldcastle's class. Always an early riser, he had done his library research early—as soon as the library opened, so he didn't see many of his fellow classmates. Still, sitting outside waiting to answer his summons to Oldcastle's private lair, Tom shuddered. When he was called in with a clipped perfunctory summons of, 'Yes, yes, come in,'

Professor Oldcastle barely looked up at him. 'Sit down,' he commanded. So, Tom nervously took a seat. 'I've heard rumors of an ugly cheating scandal going on. What do you know about it?'

"'Nothing, Professor, I get to the library early and do most of my work before most people come in. Then I leave for class.'

"'So, you've witnessed no students stealing books or hiring former students of mine to submit old papers?'

"'No, Professor, I seldom see other students there. I did see you there early last Saturday morning. I think it was just ten past seven in the morning.'

"'So it was. Dismissed.'"

71

"That's all the dude said, Dismissed? Just who the hell does this Oldcastle guy think he is?" Sly was outraged.

"'Yeah,' Pete echoed. 'Somebody needed to knock him off his high horse so he could scurry around with the rest of us.'"

Amanda asked, "So, what happened with the cheating scandal?"

Phil took out the book, volume two it was, and checked it. "Yes, there was a cheating scandal. It turned out that the very ones who were doing the cheating were Professor Oldcastle's favorite students, ones with very WASPish names. Not a one was Irish or Italian or Polish. Tom passed with a high *B*. Not even Oldcastle could justify a lower grade than that."

"Did Tom tell his wife Lexie about all that was going on?" Amanda asked.

"Well, yes and no," Phil replied.

"Ah, for real, Phil! Did he or didn't he? From what I've seen or TV it's customary for spouses to unload the weight of their workaday world on each other," Sly objected.

"Yeah, while they're cooking dinner," Pete added. "Although I don't see why they waste so much time cooking things that taste perfectly fine raw. But to each her or his own."

"No," Phil explained slowly and a bit sadly. "Lexie was spending more and more of her time 'working late' as the humans call it."

"Well, if she was spending so much time working late, she must have been bringing in more money. And more money could mean that the two of them could eat at a restaurant and wouldn't have to spend so much time cooking. I know a lot of those human restaurants have good stuff to eat. I've sampled quite a bit from the local dumpster." Pete puffed out his chest as if he were boasting—which, in fact, he was.

"Pete, sometimes I can't believe that we've eaten out of the same dumpster. Lexie wasn't really working overtime. She was making out with her boss, I bet. I was wondering when things would begin to heat up. I mean, so far things have been pretty humdrum, as they say." Sly seemed exasperated but eager to get on with the more salacious part of the tale.

"Watch the time," Carrie cautioned.

"Carrie's right, we need to get on with our little narrative," Phil agreed. Lexie and her boss were having an affair. Her boss had all the traits Tom lacked. He was moderately wealthy from defending students arrested for drug charges, mostly possession of pot with a few caught with LSD or cocaine or heroin. The parents of the college students were eager to get their sons and daughters cleared of the drug charges. Lexie's boss had profited from the fear of college students losing their deferments from the draft. If they got kicked out of school, they'd lose their protected status. Now that the draft was phasing out and the Viet Nam War winding down, he'd lose that ready source of income, so he had to find a new angle. So, he wanted to talk things over with Lexie after hours. As the two of them were sharing joint after joint of pot, they came up with an idea. He'd continue his public image as a squeaky-clean defense attorney, so his pot parties would have to remain ultra-secretive and far removed from public scrutiny. However, he would campaign for the legalization of marijuana and establish a political network that would solicit donations, especially from college students. Lexie suggested that he network with like-minded attorneys from other college towns and soon he headed a vast regional and then national organization for the Abolishment of Pot Penalties (APP, for short). But I'm getting ahead of the story. One winter evening as a snowstorm raged outside, Lexie and her boss lost themselves in the miasma of pot smoke and began groping each other. The rest is history."

"So what did Tom do?" Amanda asked

"I'm beginning to see the picture here," Sly observed. "I bet that Tom did what he usually did."

"Get a .357 magnum and catch the two in flagrante and blow them away?" Pete asked with perhaps a little too much enthusiasm.

"Pete, you've been watching way too much TV in your free time," Sly commented. "Naw, Tom probably just drowned in his troubles in his books, escaping to faraway places and times. That was probably good for his grades and all, but maybe not for himself."

"Sly, you're right, but you forgot just one other factor," Phil replied.

"Yeah, so what's that?"

"Tom lost himself in his studies all right, but he also lost himself in soccer. The simple rules of the game and just the equally simple layout of the field comforted him. At last he found an escape from arrogant professors, cheating spouses, and all of the other problems he faced, not the least of which was an ever-shrinking bank account. He played on an intramural team with an international flavor. Two Nigerians played forwards, The midfielders were a mix of Germans and Italians, two of the fullbacks were Dutch and the other two Americans, but one of those Americans had spent most of his childhood in Germany. The squad lacked an experienced goalkeeper, so Tom and the other American alternated at that position. The Nigerian forwards were fast and nimble with excellent ball skills. They boasted that when they returned home to Nigeria, they would become generals in the army and perhaps chiefs of state. 'Maybe they will,' Tom thought. The other players didn't talk much but just played with a tempered abandon. The team was good, and soon teams from other towns and states traveled to campus to play them. Tom wasn't the star of the squad by any means, but he played a good, steady form of defense that allowed the forwards and midfielders to take risks that they otherwise wouldn't have done.

"Lexie did make it to one game. The opposing team consisted of former collegiate players who had used up all of their eligibility and, like Tom's team, foreign nationals. For this match, Tom and the other American had agreed to alternate halves at fullback and goalkeeper. In the first half, Tom played wing fullback and almost scored. On an overlap, he raced down the sidelines, cut to the middle, and sent a screaming shot that bounced off the crossbar. For the rest of the half, the opposing team marked him closely and, as they say, he had a quiet time. In the second half, Tom made a few routine stops. The real excitement would take place in the two overtime periods that the teams had agreed to play. No one was content with a draw. In a move reminiscent of Tom's near miss in the first half, the opposing fullback exchanged places with a forward and sent a booming shot into the far upper corner of the goal. Tom fisted that one away. A few minutes later, Tom had to dive to his left side to stop an expertly drilled shot coming from a midfielder who had been trailing a striker. But then, in the second overtime period with only seconds remaining, the opposing team lobbed a pass over the heads of Tom's fullbacks. Tom had to race off his goal line to confront the opposing player. Tom slid down, but his opponent skillfully lofted the ball over Tom's outreached hands. Goal! Game over. After the two sides formed lines opposite each other and shook hands, a disappointed Tom slowly made his way over to the sidelines where Lexie stood. Her only two words to Tom were, 'You lost.'"

"That's it? You lost? If I wouldda been Tom, I would have kissed her goodbye and good riddance." Sly was shaking his fist at an imaginary Lexie.

"So, Phil, what became of the two?" Amanda asked. "It looks to me as if they were finished."

"They were. Lexie assumed she'd run off with her boss Mark Lawless and live happily -ever -after in some pot paradise. If the truth be told, Mr. Lawless was raking in the big bucks as director of his APP lobby. He was spending more and more time in state capitals, even in Washington, D. C., lobbying for the abolition of pot penalties. After a short while, he felt that Lexie had just burdened him with excess baggage, so he dumped her for the daughter of a liberal U. S. senator."

"What became of Lexie?' Amanda asked. She was visibly shaken by all of the human intrigue and scandal. She thought to herself, "I'm glad that my humans didn't act that way. They would have had no time for me because of all their little games. My humans pretended that they owned me, but I knew that I owned them."

"Lexie ran off and joined a commune," Phil explained. "After that Tom didn't hear of her. All he did was to file divorce papers. But Lexie was never served with the paperwork because no one could find her."

"That's a sad story," Amanda concluded. "But it seems that there were lots of sad stories then. It's like humans couldn't control their own inventions."

"What do you mean, Amanda?" Pete asked, twisting his face in utter consternation.

"Well, human scientists developed birth control pills and then humans couldn't deal with new freedom. They wanted free sex, sex without reproduction, without any consequences. And some got sick. And some got crazy."

"Yeah, but not all humans did," Sly objected.

"True," Amanda acknowledged. "But enough did so to make a difference."

"Maybe so, but I'll bet I know what Tom did," Sly added in a strange break with his habit of making off-topic comments. The guy retreated into his world of books. Maybe he was a lousy husband, but he became a hell of a student."

Relieved to be back on topic, especially since Carrie began constantly looking down at her watch, Phil for once agreed with Sly. "You're right, Sly. He finished his course work with high marks, he passed his three days of written and oral examinations with distinction, and the examining committee rapidly approved his dissertation topic. There was only one disturbing incident in his studies, and it didn't directly involve him. The incident did, however, influence his views on university life."

The recently reformed Sly couldn't contain himself. "Tom caught the head of the department having an affair with the secretary, I'll bet. I've seen stuff like that happen on TV."

"Not too far off, Sly. In Tom's last class before he took his general examination, the professor switched the location from the assigned classroom to his house just off campus. The house itself was a crumbling, ninety year old Victorian mansion. At one time some would have deemed it majestic. But age and neglect had ravaged it. The chimney badly needed tuck pointing. Tom could see that even in the dying twilight of a winter evening. The steps leading to the frame porch creaked with every step, and the paint was flecking off the entire wooden structure. Dead vines still clung to the brick, perhaps even holding the structure together in a precarious web. When Tom knocked on the door, the Professor didn't open it. Instead a fellow graduate student did. Tom had seen her before in a few of his other classes. She had rich black hair and always sported blood-red lipstick. For a moment, Tom wondered if she had had the lips permanently stained that color. She wore tight fitting jeans that and an equally tight fitting cashmere sweater that accentuated her breasts. He recalled that her name was Rachel. Tom entered and joined a small circle of a dozen students. During the class, the grad student who opened the door said nothing. The workload in the class was crushing: a twelve to fifteen page paper due every week along with a heavy reading load of seven hundred or more pages. The routine continued week after week after exhausting week. Eventually, though, the darkness of winter was starting to yield to the April sun. When the students left the house after class, they gathered together, taking in the light breezes of the spring wind. Then one student, a British woman in her mid-forties, broke the silence with one disturbing question: 'Have you noticed that, when we submit our weekly essays, Rachel has nothing to turn in?" Tom and the others reflected for a moment until someone else added the following disturbing fact. 'Not only does she not submit any essay, she also doesn't get one graded essay back.' Then the British woman posed another even more disturbing question. 'Do you note that she didn't leave with the rest of us? In fact, she never leaves. She's shacking up with the professor, no doubt for a wealth of individual tutoring on topics probably not related to our course of study.'"

"I knew it, I knew it. I knew it would come down to it. I'll bet that the 'special tutoring sessions' ended as soon as ol' Rachel got some plum job on a university campus far away. That way the old geezer of a professor could have his jollies and not even pay for them. Hell, he even had one less paper to read a week. What a scam." Sly rubbed his forepaws together in some bizarre form of voyeuristic ecstasy.

"You've got two minutes, Phil. Wind it up," Carrie cawed.

Phil nodded in agreement. "Tom's disillusionment reached its final stage when Tom overheard two women professors talking in the departmental offices. They were talking about interviewing candidates for a position that had just opened. Tom was all ears for this conversation for university jobs were becoming scarce and he hoped to get a better idea of just what faculty on the interviewing committee were looking for. One voice, an older woman's voice, grew louder as if she were broadcasting for anyone within forty feet of her could hear easily. Perhaps she was boasting. 'Well, I, for one, wouldn't even consider hiring someone—man or woman—whom I wouldn't want to sleep with.' For Tom, the alluring taste of a university job had turned bitter."

"I think I know what happened next," Amanda volunteered. "Tom would go home, for he had nowhere else to turn. He didn't have money, he didn't have a spouse, he didn't have any hopes. Maybe it was time to start over again, but in a very different direction. They say you can't go home again, but sometimes you have no other options."

"Yeah, Amanda, you're on to it. Tom had to swallow pride and humbly ask if he could return home for a while. And he had thought that he had done everything right." Phil just shook his head.

Carrie cawed loudly, "Time's up" and off she flew.

STAGE EIGHT

WORKING FOR A LIVING

THE FOLLOWING WEEK, PETE SURPRISED everyone, including himself, by being the first one to scurry into the Convocation Area. Pete started thinking out loud. "Now, what I want to know is what this Tom was doing for food all the time while Lexie was off communing or whatever. I mean, a lot of humans don't do so good being alone and all. Amanda pointed that out. Now we opossums, we can go solo or sometimes even travel around in small groups." Pete caught himself talking out loud and glanced around to see if anyone had overheard him. He had sensed a heavy, slow tread approaching closer and closer. "That's gotta be Phil coming. I'm just glad it's not Sly. If that old raccoon had heard me talkin' about opossums goin' alone, he probably would have ripped off some snide comment like, "possums go it alone because nobody can stand being around them, not even other 'possums.' When Phil comes up, I'll ask him."

In less than two minutes, an immense shadow entered the perimeter of the Convocation Area. Soon Phil himself crossed over just a few strides away from Pete. The normally placid ape stood tall and began pounding his chest fiercely. Then he abruptly stopped his chest thumping and turned to Pete. "Sometimes I just got to let loose, especially before these meetings. I go to get stuff off my chest before I play the role of the kindly, considerate narrator. You know what I mean?"

"Sure, Phil," the perturbed Pete replied, just grateful that Phil wasn't really mad, at least not at him. "Hey, Phil, something's been troublin' me."

With this remark, Phil settled into a sitting mode and looked like an immense Buddha, placid and benevolent. "Ok, Pete, what's been bugging you?"

"With Tom havin' all these troubles with Lexie and her takin' off and all, I just wondered what the guy was eating? I mean a lot of humans in similar situations eat stuff that they'd normally toss into the dumpster for the likes of Sly and me. Only humans don't really have the gastro-intestinal mustard to live on junk food all the time. So, they tend to get fat or sick or both. I think on TV I've seen some guys just start marinating themselves in booze. So, what did Tom do?"

"Well, Pete, that's a fair question. A lot of humans don't eat well and a lot of humans do drink too much booze. One morning Tom woke up and could smell his retchy self and feel his stomach churning with a stew of cheap bourbon and leftover pepperoni pizza. He couldn't stand himself. So, he made the tough decision to clean up and sober up and call home. His scholarship was running out and all he had left to do was to finish his dissertation and he could work on that at home. He had to start his change of diet by eating a whole lot of humble pie, ask his parents for help, and get a job while he finished his dissertation."

Just then Sly and Amanda walked in from different directions. "Did I hear that ole Tommy-boy finally figured it out that he'd need to get a job and make some money? It's about time the bimbo came around and smelled the persimmons, as my grampa would say."

"Sly, you weren't even around when your grandfather died, were you?" an incredulous Amanda asked.

"Well, no, that's true. I wasn't around for the passin' of my forebears. But smellin' the persimmons, that's a genuine raccoon sayin' passed around for hundreds of coon years."

Just then, Carrie swooped down from the skies and announced that it was time to start the weekly meeting.

Phil obliged as he opened the ponderous volume detailing this portion of Tom's life. "Once Tom had admitted to himself that he needed to start his life over—and that he didn't have all of the answers—he took a deep breath and called home. The response was better than he had thought. There were no 'I-told-you-so's or anything like that from Tom's mother. She told him that, of course, he was welcome back. Tom assured her that it would be for only six to eight months. By then, he thought he could save enough money to restart his life. His father welcomed him back, too, only with two conditions. 'What are they [the conditions, that is]?' Tom asked, fearing the worst. His father outlined his two, which turned out to be three conditions. 'First of all, don't bring in some girl to stay here. Swinging from one bad relationship to another won't do you any good. And getting involved romantically on the rebound can sometimes be a big mistake. Second, you can earn your keep by cutting the grass and doing some painting that I've been putting off. Last of all, you can't get drunk in my house and let yourself rot and fester in the past. You've got to look ahead to a new future, a future that you never anticipated. Agreed' Tom replied that those conditions were more than fair, so the prodigal son returned, sufficiently chastened."

"Hey, I want to know why you called Tommy the 'prodigal son'? I mean it wasn't like he was getting plastered or stoned every night or blowin' his money on prostitutes or anything." Sly punctuated his speech with an extended forepaw, almost jabbing out each word.

"True, Sly, Tom wasn't guilty of any of those things—except on the couple of occasions when he poured a little too much of that cheap bourbon down his gullet. But he had committed the most grievous error of all."

"Yeah, Phil, so what's that?" Sly demanded to know.

"Arrogance, pride, you name it."

"Yeah, well, Phil, you got me there. Tom had assumed he could do no wrong, but he really messed up. Ok, let's go on with the story."

"Yes, let's get on with it," Amanda insisted. Sometimes she found Sly to be just so annoying. Sly sensed the exasperated tone in Amanda's voice, and answered it with a sneering gaze, lips turned downward in disgust. Pete didn't want any trouble, for in his former life, he had witnessed a couple of dog / raccoon fights, vicious, snarling, bloody affairs. And he had no desire to witness such mayhem again.

Phil thumped his chest three times just to get their attention. He also fixed his gaze on Carrie and said in a low, booming voice, "Carrie, add three minutes."

Sly started to object, "But our little tiff didn't take—"

Pete asserted himself in a rare moment of aggression. "Enough, Sly, as we all agreed earlier let's get on with the story." In response, Sly sulked a bit, but that was all.

"Tom drove home in a banged up Ford Pinto that he had bought when his VW died. In a few spots where the floorboards had rusted through, he could see the road beneath him. He had used a few old license plates to cover the rusted and rotted spots. Unfortunately, he lacked a sufficient number of old plates to cover all of the spots. Unlike many of the 60's generation, Tom didn't have fond memories of his VW Bug. As he drove home, he didn't miss having to worry about vapor lock. Instead, he worried about the radiator or a hose bursting. Before he left, he had bought an inexpensive can of Stop Leaks and hoped for the best. He couldn't afford a new radiator, so, as they say, he drove home on a wing and a prayer. He also kept an eye on the temperature gauge, constantly afraid that the engine would overheat in the August heat. He recalled last winter when every night he had to take the battery out of the VW and bring it inside so that it wouldn't freeze up in the January cold. Then in the morning he'd have to reverse the process. The radio on the Pinto didn't work and he didn't have the money to replace it, so on the drive home he was left alone in his thoughts. He thought about getting his old job back as a waiter at the country club, but that wouldn't pay enough for him to save up enough money to move out of his parents' place. He'd have to start pounding the pavement, and get any job that paid enough for him to put away some cash.

"When he got home, his parents welcomed him with open arms—literally. His mom hugged him, and in a rare move so did his father. Still, it was crushing for Tom to admit such a defeat. He had failed his mother, his father, and himself. He thought. When he attended Sunday mass with his parents, he saw the names of three of his grade school friends listed on a small memorial that commemorated parishioners who had died in the service of their country. Tom blushed a bit in shame. He had opposed the war but not the ones who had served in it. Now he was alive and some of those who thought they were doing their duty were not. He felt privileged to be alive and wanted to do something worthwhile with his life, but what?

"But before he could support noble causes, he first had to support himself. He'd have to finish his dissertation, so he put aside two hours a day and all day Saturday to work on that. The rest of the time he devoted to finding a job. He studied the Want Ads in the newspaper diligently and even got some interviews, but they didn't go that well. Employers figured that Tom would quit as soon as he finished his dissertation, and they might have been right. Still, Tom recalled one interview at a janitorial service. He thought he might even get it. It paid double the minimum wage and would allow him enough time to work on his dissertation. When the interview ended, the head of the janitorial service shook hands with Tom and declared his workplace philosophy: 'Son, there's two types of people in this world. There are those who push brooms, and those who tell others how to push brooms You look to me like someone who can tell other guys how to push a broom.' Tom left after the interview, confident that he'd get the job, but he didn't. A man who had twenty years experience as a janitor got the job."

Amanda interjected her own opinion. "Well, that seems fair. A person with that much experience should get the job over someone who has no experience."

Sly mumbled something about "Miss Goody-Two-Shoes always butting in, but he kept his voice low so no one else could hear him. He just had to keep himself satisfied with his own resentment. Pete just rolled his eyes, wondering if his friend would ever change.

Phil noted the reactions of his fellows. He didn't say much, preferring to let sleeping raccoons lie." After two weeks of frustrated searching, Tom finally found a job. It was only for two months, but it would at least give him time to look for something better. It was a job in a plastics plant. The owners had just secured a major contract, but in the process had stretched the truth a bit about their ability to supply plastic refrigerator parts on short notice. Tom smiled when he recalled the famous line from *The Graduate,* 'Plastics.' He guessed that people had put their faith in the brave new world of plastics. When Tom showed up for an interview, they didn't even bother with it. They told him to get to work cutting the still hot plastic as it pushed out from an immense extrusion machine. Tom hadn't brought work gloves because he had no idea he would be hired on the spot, so after the first two hours of work his hands were raw, blistered, and bleeding. But he knew he couldn't complain or he might lose the only job he could get. At the lunch break—a full fifteen minutes—a bloodshot man in his late fifties tossed him a pair of gloves. 'Here, kid, you'll need these. Oh, and here are bandages. In a couple of days your hands will get used to it.' Tom learned later that the man with bloodshot eyes had been working eighteen hour shifts for two weeks. So, Tom labored on. The man with the bloodshot eyes had been right. After three days, Tom's hand had adjusted to the work. The gloves had helped immensely, too. Tom spent his last three dollars on a new set of work gloves and returned the ones he had been given. 'Hey, man, those were a gift. Keep 'em. Maybe you can pass them on to the next unlucky stiff who comes to work here.' Then the man took a sip from a flask he kept in his hip pocket. 'That's the only damn way I can make through these long shifts. If I drink just a sip, it keeps me goin'. If I drink more than a sip, I'll get woozy and either get fired or get hurt. And I can't afford either one. By the way, kid, get yourself another job if you can.'

"Tom thanked the veteran again, worked his shift, even did a little overtime, and awaited his first paycheck, which he picked up after three weeks on the job. On Saturday morning, he rushed to the bank to deposit the check and breathed a sigh of relief. 'Maybe now I can at least buy this week's groceries and put the rest aside.'"

"Well, that's really nice," Sly commented. "So, did he marry the boss's daughter and live happily ever after?"

Now both Amanda and Pete just glared at Sly. Even Carrie took her eyes off the watch and shot him a stare that made him feel like roadkill.

"No, Sly, Tom's euphoria had a real short life span. On the following Tuesday, Tom's bank notified him that his paycheck bounced. 'What the hell,' Tom cursed. I worked at a plastics company, not a rubber factory.' He got to work extra-early on Wednesday, and spoke to his foreman. 'Yeah, the bosses sort of forgot to deposit money in the payroll account. They also forgot one important fact in all their calculations. I mean, these guys are engineers. They're supposed to know what they're doing. They forgot that plastic shrinks when it cools. So, all that plastic you cut needs to go back into the old extrusion machine and then be cut the next day when it's cooled and can be cut to specifications. I warned them this would happen, but, oh, no, they knew better and were hell bent on delivering the parts on time. There are two semi-trucks parked by the loading dock. Start hauling out the pieces you cut and start all over again. I can't believe those two yo-yo's in the front office did this. Anyway, Tom, none of this shit is your fault. Besides, you get paid by the hour, so what's the difference?" Tom worked until his two months were up. Then he had to start looking for work all over again. None of the rest of Tom's paychecks bounced.

"Tom still entertained dreams of a college professorship. So, he steadily labored away at his dissertation and even took a week off after his plastics job ended to devote himself entirely to his magnum opus, which he admitted no one else would read except his dissertation advisor and a few unlucky others who formed his dissertation committee. At the end of the week, though, he pored over the Want Ads on the lookout for any job that would last a year and allow him to put away money. After two days of searching, he found one. He promptly called the number on the ad and got the job over the phone. The only problem was that he'd have to join the Boilermakers' Union. His initiation fee and first month's union dues would be deducted from his first paycheck. He'd need to buy himself a hardhat and steel-toed shoes, too, and be sure to wear heavy-duty, long-sleeved shirts and the sturdiest jeans he could find. He'd have to report to work the next day, Friday, and, if he wanted he could also work on Saturday. After he hung up the phone, Tom made a list of all that he'd have to buy. The jeans he had. He also dug up some long-sleeved flannel shirts from the basement. He'd have to buy his hardhat and get an old pair of hiking boots a steel toe-cover. Glumly, he figured that his first paycheck would be mighty slim"

"This is rich," gloated Sly. "The kid's gonna have to pay to work. I love it."

"He's lucky to have the ability to pay. Some people don't have that luxury," Amanda interjected rather snappishly as she was tiring of Sly's constant interruptions. So was Pete. So was Carrie. And so was Phil. Sly looked around for some support. There was none, so he rather sheepishly whispered, "Sorry."

Phil shifted his eyes form Sly to the volume in front of him. "So Tom outfitted himself for work and arrived early, as he usually did when he felt his nerves jangling and jostling with each other. In order to get to work, he had to enter through a tunnel about eighty feet long. Above it, the morning traffic—mostly trucks at this time of day—thundered their way. Graffiti covered the walls, but the morning light was dim, and dust and grit and grease had smeared over whatever message the spray-painted murals might have had. Beneath Tom's feet, equally filthy discarded fast-food wrappers and some brown-black puddles of dubious origin pooled. At every other step, Tom could hear the crunch of broken glass. He reported to a one-room rusting steel shed whose white paint was flecking off, leaving a score or more of rust pimples over the surface. 'So, you the new guy?' a voice in the corner cried out. 'You're early. That's a good sign.' The man in the corner stood up and took a step towards Tom. 'I'm Slim, your foreman.' Slim was anything but. He stood about six feet two inches tall and had a massive beer belly hanging over his jeans. When he extended his arm to shake Tom's hand, Tom could see the rippling muscles of his forearm as the sleeves were rolled up. His hand felt rough and calloused and even a bit scratchy as it clamped down on Tom's like a vise. He smiled in a friendly way, showing a few gaps where teeth had either been broken out or taken out. 'You're new to this kind of work, aren'tcha?' Tom wondered if his rawness was that evident. 'I could tell by your boots. Well, you've got the steel toes, so I guess that'll do. Anyway you're gonna have a tough first day. Your job will be to carry over twenty-five and forty-five pound steel plates over to the furnaces over yonder. Then wait until the metal is white-hot and use these tongs to carry the heated metal over to the punch press machines for bending. Here, take these heavy-duty gloves and these tongs and a pair of these safety glasses. You'll sweat like a mother, so be sure to take a few salt pills every couple of hours. Good luck! A lot of guys don't last much long at this work.' Tom replied that he'd work through the pain because he needed the money. 'Yeah, well, don't we all, kid. Don't we all.'

"Tom enjoyed a few moments of rest before the rest of his team slowly eased their way back to work. The man who operated the punch press was nicknamed Coon-Face because a black ring of oil and grease circled his eyes. Tom later learned that his colleagues hoisted that nickname on him because he did, in fact, have black rings around his eyes where the safety goggles ended and his skin of his face began. It was rumored that ole Coon-Face bathed only once a month because the rings stayed in place for at least four weeks. Then they mysteriously disappeared. But Coon-Face could see to it that the heavy iron plates were bent exactly to specifications, never more than a millimeter off and even then those occasions when he was off were rare. His companion, 'Possum, derived his name from his studied slothfulness. His job was to steady the heated metals in place while Coon-Face checked the templates. But he didn't do much steadying—"

"Hey, wait a minute here, Phil. I'm beginning to detect a clear pattern of discrimination here. I recoil in indignation at the thought of a greasy faced human being called 'Coon-Face.' This is a clear affront to every raccoon in the world. As is the insinuation that all 'possums are lazy even though Pete here can, in fact, be pretty lazy at times." Sly punctuated his speech with his upraised paws, claws extended menacingly, pummeling the air against some invisible foe.

"Well, you do have black rings around your eyes, Sly. It could be worse. They could call female raccoons 'bitches.'" Amanda countered.

"Ah, humans are so dumb that they can't even tell a male raccoon from a female one." Sly had turned his head away and was muttering on and on."

"Point taken," Phil said to Sly and Pete. "But I can't change what was said."

"Yeah, yeah, all right. Let's get on with it." Sly answered.

Phil regarded Sly's last reaction as a minor triumph. "Well, the foreman was right. Tom had a tough day of it. For the first hour, Tom sweated and drenched himself in sweat as he hauled the twenty-five and forty-five pound plates over to the press and set them down to meet their fate at the hands of Coon-Face. In two hours, he felt a little taxed so he downed some salt pills as his foreman had directed. By lunchtime, he was sitting down in complete exhaustion to gobble down his bologna and cheese sandwich and apple. 'Next time,' Tom vowed, 'I'll bring about a gallon of water to wash down the food. And replace what I've sweated out. I can't go running to the drinking fountain every ten minutes.' The foreman strolled over and told Tom's team that they could enjoy a break because they had to wait for more orders to come down from the shop office. They couldn't just lounge around, though. He had them clean up their area. Still, that work was a welcome break from scurrying over to the furnace and back again with white-hot iron plates. Later in the afternoon, Tom went back to hustling white-hot iron plates from the furnace to the press. When the foreman announced that they could resume their work, Tom gritted his teeth in fearful anticipation. Strangely, though, he found the task less stressful, although he still downed several salt pills. 'At least,' Tom reflected, 'the sweat keeps the grease and coal dust from the nearby Peabody Coal plant from staining my face. At least, I won't end up looking like old Coon-Face.'"

"I repeat my objection to the humans impugning the physical features of raccoons," Sly interjected.

"Point taken, Sly," Phil responded. Then Phil continued. "When the whistle blew to end their shift, 'possum asked Tom if he was coming back. 'Will we be seeing you on Monday, Kid? You had a pretty tough first day.' Tom responded that he was coming back tomorrow. 'Workin' on Saturday, huh. Well, that's good. My buddy and I will be back, too. Gotta get some of that overtime money. Workin' on Saturday ain't so bad. Hardly any of the big bosses and foremen show up, so we sortta determine our own pace. Well, see ya tomorrow, Gotta pick up my paycheck.' Tom wouldn't receive his first paycheck for another two weeks so he made his way to the tunnel that led to the world outside.

"When Tom exited, he spied the tunnel lined with two opposing rows of women. They looked hard and battle-weary, their eyes drained of life and their cigarettes dangling from their lips. They bore little resemblance to the seductive prostitutes selling their wares on film and television. Their clothes were revealing, but what they revealed didn't entice Tom at all. His eyes must have flashed his disapproval, for one of the women shouted out at him: 'Ya think you're better than us, huh. Well, ya ain't. We're all in this same rat-hole together.' As Tom paced his way through the gauntlet of women lining the tunnel, he tried to keep his eyes straight ahead. He did hear one voice yelling out. 'Hey, just leave the kid alone. He ain't got no paycheck. Must be his first week here. He'll soon get around to seein' how things are around here.' Tom was beginning to see how none of his graduate studies had prepared him for the world he was experiencing for the first time.

"After he started up his clunker of a car and had made his way halfway home, though, he looked back on his university experience. He recalled the conversation he had overheard in the departmental offices, the one in which one professor had casually remarked that she wouldn't consider hiring anyone she wouldn't consider sleeping with. 'Maybe the two worlds aren't so different, after all. Maybe I had blinders on and just wasn't seeing what was really going on. Then he remembered, too, the graduate student who had shacked up with the professor. 'The more things change, the more they stay the same,' Tom concluded.

One constant remained. Tom would never get a university teaching job. When he got home, he showered, set the clothes washer going with his work clothes, and readied himself for the dinner his father had cooked—hamburgers and a salad—he felt relieved. Then, he went through the day's mail. 'Two more rejection letters,' he sighed. 'Well, I can add them to the growing mountain of rejections. I'm going to have to look elsewhere.' He tossed out the two rejections letters he had received today, paused for a moment, and then took all of the dozens of rejection letters he had received in the last few months. 'It's time to start over,' he judged. So, he scanned the Want Ads listing by listing, not ruling out any possibility until finally his eyes fixed on one: 'Wanted, English Teacher and Soccer Coach for the Next School Year.' Now Tom felt energized. 'I can do that. I'll have to get my teaching certification, but, if I start on that right away, I can at least show that I'll be more than halfway to getting my credentials completed by the time school starts next August.' He revised his resume, wrote a letter, and prayed that both would work.'"

"Well, Phil, did they?" Amanda asked. She still felt deeply troubled by the hard lives of women who had sold their bodies. She also knew of dogs that had been abused, neglected, and left out in the cold. She had no ill-will towards anyone, human or canine.

"Amanda, you'll see next week," Phil concluded.

Carrie just squawked, "Time's up."

STAGE NINE

RENEWAL AND MISGIVINGS

"Tom's prayers were answered," Phil intoned. "He interviewed, got the job, and felt he had been reborn in a manner of speaking. All he had to do was to continue working to make money, continue work on his dissertation, and at least get half of the requirements for teacher certification complete— and all before next August."

"You know," Sly intoned with grave solemnity, stroking his chin with his right forepaw, "sometimes ya got to be careful what you pray for 'cause ya might just get it."

"Aw, Sly, give the guy a break. He knows he screwed up, and it ain't like he's just loungin' on his parents' basement sofa just bein' a lot of dead weight." Pete countered, not even bothering to conceal his distaste for his former buddy.

"Yeah, Pete, at least he's not like—"

"Amanda didn't allow Sly to complete his analogy, fully realizing that it would only result in more pointless bickering. "Sly, we're supposed to be focusing the discussion on Tom, not on each other."

Phil leaned back in relief, but had one clenched fist ready to do some chest pounding just in case, Sly directed a sneer at Amanda, the left side of his lip starting to curl up in contempt, but he kept his mouth shut. Amanda reared back and set her paws down firmly as if ready to pounce. Soon the sneer faded as Sly realized that no one would back him if it came down to a fight. Suddenly the mood changed, and all four sat attentive, eyes set straight ahead, waiting for Phil to start his summary of the next chapter in Tom's life. For a few seconds, Phil sat calmly and serenely, like some Buddha figure. He thought, "You know, you've got to give Amanda credit for taking charge." Then he directed an electrifying glare that struck like a thunderbolt, first at Sly and then, far less menacingly at the other three. "All right, my friends, it's time to get down to business. Carrie, please restart the clock. We've got to do some of our own renewing."

"As you requested, Phil," Carrie replied, gazing intently at her watch.

"This time," Phil boomed out, "Tom had learned at least one lesson. He wouldn't try to go it alone, confident that he had all the answers. Instead he sought out mentors. And he soon found them. He reflected that he leaned more from them than from all of university Education professors.

"His department chair, Father Wright, a veteran of thirty years in the classroom would serve as his primary mentor. He was a slender balding Jesuit with horn-rimmed glasses, so he looked every bit the scholar in his long, flowing black robe. He was fluent not only in English and Latin but in French and German as well. He had immersed himself in Medieval literature but also read contemporary fiction avidly and had a keen interest in it. His philosophy of teaching consisted of only three basic principles. 1) Prepare each class as if it lasted not for one hour but two. Don't allow for extended, so-called pregnant pauses. Such breaks allow some of the more sophomorically cynical students time to plot against you. And at first they will test you. Make sure you pass this first test. 2) No matter how ludicrous a question may seem, don't respond sarcastically to it. If the question is genuine, all you have accomplished with sarcasm is to embitter the student against you. If the apparently ridiculous question is designed to test you, a sarcastic response just spawns another sarcastic response, and you lose control of the class in return. On the other hand, if the question indicates that the student has been inattentive, simply respond firmly and redirect the student. Sometimes you should make notes in your grade book for those consistently off-task. 3) Return tests and essays quickly, the next day if at all possible. No one wants to play a game and find out weeks later if they have won or lost. If the assignment has any instructional value, the students need to learn as quickly as possible what they have done well and what they still don't understand. Be sure to find the good as well as the bad, and whatever you do, don't try to correct every single mistake. Concentrate the corrections on only a few essential points. No one likes to be overwhelmed with negative comments. Remember that they're still learning and that no one can ingest every thing at once. Students need to digest learning in small chunks. Otherwise they choke on it. And above all else, shed the guise of the arrogant professor. Get rid of it as if it were rotting, fetid dead fish. Students get one whiff of that odor and they're gone. Teach your students but also learn from them."

"Sounds like good advice," Amanda asserted, nodding her head in Sly's direction.

"I've never been in a classroom, human or animal," Sly confessed, "not even on a scouting mission for food. But, yeah, those principles seem all right to me. Of course, the tough part lies in carryin' 'em out. I mean some kids, especially smart ones, can be hard to deal with."

"Yeah, Sly, good point." Pete concurred.

Amanda and Phil shared the same thought, but they both kept it to themselves. They felt like saying, "You should know, Sly," but prudently said nothing.

Phil resumed, turning to a new page in the massive volume. "Sly was right. Abstract principles are well and good, but real actions matter. When Tom dealt with his first set of essays, he felt overwhelmed, despairing of ever getting through all of them. His mentor anticipated his frustration. 'Remember, Tom, focus on just commenting on a few core ideas. The students aren't writing for publication. They're writing to fulfill an assignment. They're still learning, and so are you. You've got to direct all of your energy to zeroing in on the clear focus of the assignment. Keep it simple. Sometimes teachers drown in a deluge of essays because they've never clearly defined the precise purpose and goal of the assignment in the first place. Ask yourself what instructional goal, what purpose, does the assignment have.'"

"Tom still struggled with implementing the advice. The first round of essays took him hours and hours to finish. He became even more disheartened when his mentor advised him to give students the option of re-writing their essays. Tom's shoulders drooped in despair at the thought of having to re-read scores of assignments. Sensing his dejection, Father Wright offered this consolation. 'Don't worry, Tom, not all of the students will revise their work. Furthermore, you'll be able to read the revised essays far more quickly than you went through the first drafts.' Tom stared straight ahead in apparent disbelief. Nevertheless, Father Wright continued, this time a little more sternly. 'Tom, you should know by now that we learn from our mistakes, not our successes.' Reluctantly and somewhat skeptically, Tom followed the advice. To his surprise and delight, he found that his mentor had been right all along. He and Father Wright worked well together in every way but one. Tom's mentor in teaching didn't like the fact that Tom was also hired to coach. From his thirty years of experience in teaching, Father Wright had encountered far too many teachers who had channeled all of their energies into coaching. 'Whatever you do, Tom, don't become one of those jock-sniffers. You know the type who fawns over athletes, all the while forgetting that athletic glory fades quickly. You should know the lines from A. E. Housman's poem *To an Athlete Dying Young: Now you will not swell the rout / Of lads that wore their honors out.* Nothing is worse than the ex-jock except the ex-jock who is still festering in the stench of long-dead glory—or illusions of glory.'"

"Despite the misgivings of his department chair, Tom did, in fact, start coaching. In fact, he met the boys who aspired to make the team before he met his classes. Practice began in the middle of August but classes wouldn't start for two more weeks. Because of his department chair's misgivings, Tom wondered what he had signed up for. The oft quoted—or misquoted expression—'Winning isn't everything; it's the only thing'—drifted through his mind. But again he sought out a mentor. He worked with the JV squad, freshmen and sophomores, so he sought out advice from the varsity coach, a legendary figure who was destined for the high school Hall of Fame. 'You've got to regard coaching as teaching and teaching as coaching,' Matt Coughlin advised him. 'You prepare classes; you plan practices. Nothing is worse than having players standing around twiddling their thumbs just waiting for the coach to make up his mind about what to do next. By the same token, you've got to be flexible. If a practice drill you carefully planned isn't working, scrap it and move on. Listen to your players. Often, they're the best assistant coaches you'll ever have. In your case, they'll be the only assistants you'll have.'

"So, out in the August heat, Tom took this advice. Still, it's one thing to listen to a mentor and think you're heeding the advice and quite another to put that advice into practice. After one particular grueling session in which candidates for the team began practice with a two mile run, then did forty-five minutes of drills, and then scrimmaged for two hours. Tom barked out instructions to aspiring players who were all too eager to oblige. But, even Tom realized that this spurt of enthusiasm would wane once he made the final cuts. Unfortunately, some boys would be disappointed. Fifty-four were trying out for eighteen positions on the squad, so they played with intensity. Matt Coughlin looked on for a while, saying nothing. Then he quietly stepped over to Tom and during a water break and gave him some more advice. 'Tom, I know you're probably doing your best to train your boys, But you've got to remember that they're just that—boys. Most will never play soccer after high school—except maybe in some low-key recreational league. Most of the kids I teach will never put into practice the trigonometry they learn in my classroom. But they will learn to think and to reason. Those are the skills that will carry them further even if they never tackle a trig problem again. So, what skills and beliefs do you want your players to learn? Think about it before you give me some pre-cooked string of clichés. Think, too, about the disappointed thirty-six or so boys who won't make the team. What will they learn? Always place the needs of your students first. The rest will take care of itself.' After the varsity coach walked over to the varsity field, Tom admitted to himself that he had focused on the quality of the game and his own success more than on the learning outcomes for his players. Of course, it didn't help when he set out for practice, and an assistant principal yelled out: 'We're with you, Tom, all the way, win or tie.'

"By October, Tom and his team found themselves in the mid-season doldrums. So far, they had more than a winning record; they had a great record with nine wins as against only one loss—and that was a close overtime loss—and one tie. Tom knew better than to congratulate himself on being a great coach; he recognized that he had great players and for the most part he let them play their own game. Matt Coughlin had also warned him about overcoaching. 'Listen at least as much as you talk,' he cautioned Tom. And Tom made a point of listening. Still, in mid-season, the boys seemed lethargic: too many drills, too much conditioning, too many games. They were just going through the motions. So, yet once again, Tom consulted his mentor. 'Tom, you've got to make it fun. Instead of having the boys just start practice with a run, do something different. Play Capture the Flag or something. You've got to vary the pace and intensity of your workouts. Nobody goes at 110 %—not even a 100 %

for very long. The kids bang up their knees and shins when they drill and scrimmage too much. Both you and they have to learn when to relax and when to give it your all.'

"Tom started having fun both in the classroom and on the practice field. He had started as a stern taskmaster because he felt he had to if he wanted to be taken seriously, Now it was time to loosen up a little and be human. Tom had no other time to relax a bit, for when he wasn't teaching or preparing classes or practices or grading papers, he was working on his dissertation and taking the courses required for teacher certification. Still, he had never felt happier."

"Ya know, sometimes you're the happiest when you're the busiest," Sly observed, extending his right forepaw for emphasis When you're hustlin' and hustlin' there and doing this and doing that, you feel like you're worth something, like you matter. Besides, when I'm not doin' something, that's when I get into trouble."

Amanda started to respond but reconsidered and thought, "I wonder if Sly is on the brink of self-knowledge."

Pete had been listening intently, turning his head slightly upwards and sideways to hear better. "You've got a point, Sly, but you know the kid may just be overdoing it a bit. Just like that coach-guy said, ya can't go 100 % all the time. Tom may just end up spinnin' his head and walkin' in circles before he crashes to the ground. Rest is every bit as important as exercise, physical or mental. As for me, I know when I've had enough and take it easy."

Once again, Amanda had to check herself from lashing out with some sarcastic comment that wouldn't do any good. "Sly and Pete are just who they are," she reasoned. All this while Carrie just stared at her watch, but Phil broke into a faint smile and stroked his chin with the fingers of his left hand while his right hand held onto the book of Tom's life.

When Phil sensed that his colleagues had all had their say, he resumed his summary. "There's something else to add to this chapter in Tom's life. He did find some peace and tranquility."

"Did he start smokin' joints?" Sly burst out. He had been reserved for too long and couldn't contain himself.

Phil let out a sigh and forced himself to answer that question as calmly and as objectively as he could. "No, Sly, he found comfort in the weekly mass at school. It remained the one time in his schedule when he could reflect on the meaning of it all. Caught up in the race to find the money and means to support himself, he otherwise had little time to wonder about the purpose of it all. The time for prayer and reflection gave him perspective. He also learned one other important lesson."

"What's that, Phil?" Amanda asked, tilting her head sideways as she strained to understand the next phase of Tom's growth.

"Amanda, you asked a very important question," Phil replied while Sly almost broke into a cynical sneer, his upper lip rising in derision. Phil ignored—well, almost ignored—Sly's reaction as he resumed, all the while fixing a burning gaze at Sly. There was no question about the unstated meaning of that glare. "After the soccer season, when Tom at least had that job over for the year, he was assigned to monitor students as they did volunteer work at hospitals, homeless shelters, chronic care facilities, schools, and other places that used volunteers to assist them make life better for those unable to take care of themselves either temporarily or permanently. At first, Tom questioned why the school would, as he thought, take a detour from its primary mission of educating students in academic subjects and focus on this volunteer work. Tom told himself that professionals in social work and in health and welfare were better suited to assist the needy. Nevertheless, as part of his duties, he drove to different locations to check on students volunteering in hospitals, shelters, and schools."

"What changed Tom's mind?" Amanda inquired.

"Experience, that's all it took. Tom first visited a veterans' hospital. Set high on a hill, the building loomed over the entire neighborhood. A brick fence surrounded the drab brown brick building on three sides. On the east end, the Mississippi churned its brown waters. It was January, and all the leaves were gone and all looked somber. The few remaining leaves lay scattered on the ground, some frozen, others sodden with winter rains. All looked bleak, desolate, and barren."

Startling everyone else, Carrie cased out, "That's my kind of time and place." Then she settled back into her customary silence.

"Tom drove up to the front of the building, parked in the Visitors' Lot— but there weren't any other visitors—walked up the huge stone stairs, buzzed to be allowed in, signed in by a clerk who simply pointed to the register. Tom noticed that only seven other visitors had signed in over the last two weeks. Then the clerk just as taciturn as ever pointed him down the pea-green hallway. Finally, he broke his own self-imposed silence. "You'll find that high school kid down there. He's changing bedpans." Tom faked enthusiasm and strode down the hall imperiously.

"When he spied the student, Luke Matthews, he noticed that Luke was working with a doctor who bent over the prone patient, an elderly man with greasy grey hair splayed over a pillow. The doctor was cleaning out a bedsore that ran to the man's bone. Tom feared that he had intruded where he didn't belong, that he might have violated patient confidentiality. But the doctor just turned to him and said, 'Luke's doing a fine job. He jokes with the patients, old, worn out guys who for the most part don't have any visitors. This poor man had suffered alone in his house until he was evicted. That's when he was shipped off to us. Luke lets him win at cards.'

"'The hell he does,' the patient yelled out, turning his face to the side. 'I beat him fair and square every time. Damn it, Doc, watch what you're doin.' That's my ass you're dealin' with!" Luke just grinned.

"Tom grinned back. But he reflected that the roles had been reversed. Here he was the student and Luke was the teacher. 'I guess I haven't seen a lot of things,' Tom reflected, feeling guilty over his own self-imposed blinders.

"Tom's next visit sent him to monitor a student, Jaime Sanchez, who was tutoring students in a mostly Hispanic parish, located in the low rent district of town. As he turned into the school parking lot, he had to admit that the quality of the graffiti he had seen on the on the drive amazed him. Of course, he didn't have time to do much more than scan the dazzling display of bright red and oranges and yellows and blues. Even the greens impressed him as anything but institutional. The paintings livened up the otherwise fading red and brown brick of buildings that had seen Irish, then Italian, then Polish, and now Hispanic immigrants. He wondered if his own grandparents had once lived in the neighborhood. He took his time walking into Our Lady of Victory School. He checked in at the principal's office, a small room crammed with supplies stacked around a small desk where a secretary smiled as she checked him in. The classrooms looked much as they had a generation ago: wooden floors polished until they gleamed, wooden desks with a writing surface on top and a shelf below to store paper, pens, pencils, crayons, and other supplies. The wooden seat showed the wear of use, and below it was storage space for books. All was plain and simple, functional. The school had made some concessions to modern technology: all of the classrooms Tom passed had smartboards and a projector, and in two of the five classrooms he had passed students were working with Chrome books. Still, the look and feel reminded Tom of his own elementary experience."

"Ya know, Tom's little trip down memory lane reminds me of some important lessons." Sly turned suddenly serious as he nodded his head downward under the weight of a new insight. "Ya know, sometimes people just take sides and say the new is all good and the old is all bad, or sometimes folks reverse it and claim the old is all good and the new is all bad. But, ya know, things just ain't that simple. Take teaching for example. I bet the students really learn some neat stuff with those computers and those projectors. They can see images of places they'd never seen or things they'd never learn even with a thousand trips to the library. On the other hand, some of the old style stuff is important. Some stuff ya just gotta know, like the times table. Let's say ya got nine cans of sardines with thirty tasty sardines packed into each one of them, so ya gotta know pronto how many sardines each of your nine buddies gets. Ya just gottta know pronto."

"So, Sly, just how many sardines does each of your buddies get?" Pete asked, licking his lips. "I am one of your buddies, right?"

"Sure, Pete. You're one of my buddies most of the time, and you'd get twenty-seven of the tasty morsels if I had them to give to ya."

Amanda had to stifle a laugh, and even Phil grinned at Sly's little arithmetic lesson. "Still, this is a lot better than what we usually get from Sly," Phil reflected. Then Phil resumed his story. "Tom finally saw Jaime at the classroom at the very end of the long, straight corridor. He was sitting next to a middle-school aged boy. Catching a glimpse of Tom walking in, Jaime stood up and greeted him: 'Hi, coach, glad to see you.' Jaime had played on the varsity soccer team and recognized Tom. 'This is Luis. I'm helping him with ratio and proportion problems and his English grammar. Luis, this is one of my teachers.' The boy about six inches shorter than Jaime stood up and looked confused. He turned towards Jaime and said, 'I didn't know teachers had teachers.' Jaime answered by explaining that we're all teachers and learners, and sometimes we switch roles. Luis seemed satisfied or at least satisfied enough to turn back to his work. 'I want to finish this stuff so I can go out to recess,' the boy explained. Taking that comment as his cue to leave, Tom shook Jaime's hand, turned and left.

"When Tom reported back to school, he heard a buzz in the office. The president of the school, whose main job consisted of raising money in order to keep tuition low, was leaving his position. People were shocked. Father Brennan had been so successful at fund raising that tuition hadn't increased at all in the last ten years, and the scholarship fund had doubled in size. The buzz was that he was being promoted. And he was. In a brief faculty meeting after school, Father Brennan waltzed in, all smiles. Everyone expected him to announce that he was moving over to the university to direct its expansion fund. The staff quieted down as he slowly strode over to the podium, grinning all the while. 'I understand that rumors are flying about that I'm being promoted.' Here he paused to survey the grim expression on the faces in front of him before he resumed. 'And those rumors are correct. I am being promoted.' He paused again. 'But not in the way you might be thinking. I've always considered teaching and learning to be the primary mission of a school. And I've been away from those two functions for a decade. It's time to get back to the primary mission of the school. I'm being promoted all right. I'll be teaching Philosophy and Latin next year; so, if you had hoped that you wouldn't be seeing my funny face any more, you'll be disappointed.'

"Tom was stunned as were other staff. Most people assumed that administrators all scrambled for power and prestige. That's just the way it was. But here was this highly successful administrator voluntarily going back to teaching. People looked about for some hint of a major failure, a devastating miscue, but found none. Apparently Father Brennan meant what he said. Later in his career, Tom would never experience another administrator who so valued teaching and learning. Tom reflected on the origin of the term principal. The word had meant the principal teacher, in the decades before teachers and administrators were stratified into separate layers with rigid separations between—like officers and enlisted soldiers in the military, or aristocrats and serfs in Medieval times. The whole staff was reeling in delight.

"A month later, the whole staff was also reeling—this time not in delight but in stupefied disbelief and anger. The principal of the school had on a warm March weekend been arrested for soliciting in a Men's Room in a city park. Once again, a principal was leaving—but this time not voluntarily. Tom didn't know what to make of the whole sordid episode."

"Time's up," Carrie announced with a flutter of wings that sent her aloft.

STAGE TEN

RENEWAL AND MISGIVINGS, PART II

"OUTWARDLY, ALL SEEMED WELL FOR Tom," Phil read at the start of the next session.

"Oh, yeah, I get it," Sly smirked. "Next you're gonna tell us that old Tom-boy here suffered inwardly, experiencing existential angst or some such human drivel."

"I'll betcha that Tom suffered from a lack of sleep. I mean he was juggling his teaching and coaching along with finishing his dissertation and then takin' care of those courses for teacher certification. The dude has got to be worn out." Pete added this comment before he indulged in a quick possum nap.

"Aw, the kid is still young. He can handle it. It's sort of like a rite of passage or somethin' like that." Sly maintained his superior and rather flippant attitude, waving his right forepaw as if brushing away flies.

"I don't know, but I think two things really are troubling Tom," Amanda countered. "First, everything was going so well at school. That is, until the scandal involving the principal. I think that came out about the same time as the sex scandal involving cover-ups about priests and sex abuse. You know, dogs have a keen insight about these things. Some of the most abusive dog owners are all treats and lovey-dovey pats on the head in public. They're the kind who say they love all animals and then, boom, in private they chain us down and leave us out in the cold to starve. No, things are not always as they seem."

"I know what ya mean, Amanda. Why one night I was helping myself to some tasty chickens in some guy's henhouse. Later I learned that the guy had a rep for being one of those animal lovers. Well, anyway, he blasted away a time with a pump-action shotgun and all because I was just going shopping for dinner." Sly was shaking his head in disgust.

"Maybe so, Sly. But I'll also bet that Tom had another thing bothering him. I'll bet that that other factor also kept him up at night. But perhaps we should let Phil tell us about what wasn't going well for Tom." Amanda stared at Sly icily. Even Pete noticed that. Carrie just glanced down at her watch.

"Thanks, Amanda. You're right. Let's pick up the narrative. Tom was troubled by the sex scandals. I guess he forgot that all humans are flawed. He also felt very flawed himself. One reason he could throw himself into his work was that he still felt guilty about his failed first marriage. It was a mistake from the outset, and he realized that a lot of the blame lay squarely on him. While he didn't have any time to think over the past, while he was teaching, coaching, writing, and studying, he didn't have time to think things over. But by June, the school year was winding down. He completed multiple revisions of his dissertation and scheduled his oral defense of it. All he had left to do was to complete his student teaching over the summer."

"Whoa, slow down, Phil. What's this about student-teaching? Didn't Tom complete his first year of teaching? Why does he have to do student teaching? Aren't you supposed to complete that before ya get a teaching job?" Sly shook his head in bewilderment.

"In an ideal world, Tom would have done his student teaching first, before he took the job. But he got a waiver since he was enrolled in education courses. But now he had to teach for free. In fact, he had to pay tuition in order to do his student teaching."

"Wait a minute, Phil. You're telling me that he had to pay to work? Humans are wackier than I thought. If he had done a decent job teaching, then that shoudda counted for the student teaching, right. Anyways, this just looks like some kind of a scam deal. I guess it's good for the place that reaps in the tuition money, but I don't see what other good it does." Sly adamantly objected, once again shaking his head in bewilderment. "I'll never understand humans. They are a strange breed."

"Surprisingly, Sly, the student teaching turned out well for Tom," Phil commented flatly.

"What? No way," Sly objected.

"Sly, just let Phil finish," Amanda snapped.

"Yeah, Sly, let's get on with it," Pete added groggily as he was just waking up from dozing off.

Sensing that he was outnumbered, Sly retreated into a curled up ball of fur. Pausing briefly, Phil resumed. "Tom had two weeks off before his summer school student teaching would start. One week he spent traveling back to his grad school and finishing his oral defense of his dissertation. His dissertation advisor treated him to a lunch at the Faculty Club and made a point of calling him 'Doctor Albright.' Tom was pleased, but somehow this victory rang hollow. Because of a job market so tight that it squeaked, Tom figured he'd never get a university job. 'Besides,' he thought, 'I've got enough of a challenge just teaching and coaching. I should learn to do those well. As Father Wright said it takes five years before you earn your paycheck as a teacher.'

"When Tom returned from his successful defense, his parents were proud and beamed when as they called their son 'Doctor.' Tom joked that he hadn't healed anyone yet. But the joke was no laughing matter, for Tom realized that he needed healing himself. He fell into depression in the week just before summer school. He planned his classes carefully, devoting seven to nine hours a day on that task. He'd move out of his parents' place next October when he didn't have tuition to pay, so he still had the rest of his waking hours to fill. He started running again, so that exercise kept his mind off his troubles at least for another hour a day. But he still had time on his hands, even two hours of free time seemed like an eternity of too much. His mind wandered back to the conversation he had heard in the departmental lounge, the one in which two professors bragged of not hiring anyone they wouldn't sleep with. Although that incident occurred months and months ago, it still left a faint, fetid stench in his mind. And now there was this sex scandal with the principal and with the cover-up of abuse. It seemed that everyone was going sex crazy. But then Tom had to admit that he wasn't immune from the insanity, nor could he get off by shoveling the blame on institutions. People, himself included, made up the institutions. For more than a few moments, he sat paralyzed with indecision. Just what should he do next?

"He flipped on music by the Rolling Stones just to busy himself and lose his thoughts in the frenzied beat of the music, but even that didn't work. He listened to one song in particular, 'Paint It, Black' over and over again as the lyrics haunted him:

> I see the girls walk by
> Dressed in their summer clothes
> I have to turn my head
> Until my darkness goes
>
> . . .
>
> I look inside myself
> And see my heart is black.

"Now, this getting interesting," Sly burst out, almost bounding out of his short-lived hibernation. "It looks as if this Tom-kid is gonna have his own sex scandal to worry about. So, Phil, what happened? Did Tom go out and have orgy after orgy. Tell me the details. Inquiring minds want to know."

"I don't want to disappoint you, Sly, but it didn't go down in that direction although some romance was involved," Phil responded.

"Romance, shomance, I just want the raw sex. You know gimmee, gimmee some satisfaction," Sly admitted.

Amanda looked up as if saying she wanted relief from Sly's outbursts.

"Well, you're going to be a little disappointed, Sly," Phil commented. "Tom wasn't about to throw himself into one bad relationship after he was still recuperating from his first mistake. Perhaps for a few, sex can be utterly physical with no emotional bonds binding people together. Sometimes those bonds are made of soft velvet and sometimes they're made of cold, hard steel, but for most the emotional attachments are there, good or bad. Well, anyway, back to the story."

At this point, Sly and Pete were dozing off, half listening, half sleeping. For the moment, Phil ignored them.

"Tom had to complete his student-teaching to fulfill his requirements for teacher certification. To meet those demands, he had to do his work in a large, urban public school not far from where he had taught in the regular school year. So, he dutifully enrolled, dutifully and painfully paid his tuition, and then prepped for his courses. One class was designed for students who had failed freshman English; the other for students who wanted to get ahead. As you might guess, Tom would be teaching both ends of the spectrum, so he had to plan accordingly. He figured that most of the students in the remedial class had failed because of absenteeism, indifference, self-abuse as in drugs or alcohol or parental neglect and possibly abuse. So, he focused on making the course as appealing as he could while still meeting academic standards. When he met with his supervising teacher, she was sipping coffee in the Faculty Lounge. 'You're that Tom guy, right. And I see you've already been teaching for a year. I don't want to get in your way, so, if you want to ask a question, you can find me here.' Tom quickly determined that she didn't want to plan with him, that she had absolutely no intention of ever entering the classroom, and, of course, that she would be paid, and he wouldn't. He figured that this would be six weeks he'd have to get through on his own. He was right."

"So, what does any of this have to do with romance?" Amanda asked. Sly and Pete had lapsed into a deep sleep, as made evident by Sly's snoring.

"This is where he met the woman who would turn out to be his one, true love." By this time, Pete, too, was snoring and rolled over on top of Sly, who woke up and bellowed, "Get your possum ass off me." Phil glared and advanced two steps towards the sleeping uglies. Sly nudged Pete and the two soon sat and looked like contrite schoolboys, heads upraised, ears straight up like radio towers, all giving the appearance of dutiful attention.

"As I was saying," Phil resumed pronouncing each word slowly and deliberately, calculating the attentiveness of his two penitents. "For the moment, they would give him no more trouble," Phil judged, so he picked up the narrative where he had left off. "In the classroom next to his, another student teacher found herself in charge of the class. Her supervising teacher (ST), her supposed mentor, had also stationed herself in the Faculty Lounge, undoubtedly sipping coffee with Tom's ST, Tom thought that she looked familiar, that he must have seen her before but, if so, only for a moment. 'If I had met her before, I wouldn't have forgotten her.' He had to catch himself, for he was slipping into what he feared was a trap, the one that had gotten him into romantic trouble the first time. She stood about five foot-four with an athletic build. 'She must have been and probably still is, an athlete,' Tom concluded. She sported short, blonde hair, prominent cheekbones, deep dark brown eyes, a petite nose, and a wide smile. Tom had lost himself in her eyes and lips. He had to shake himself free for the trap his own mind was springing. She dressed modestly in loose-fitting white blouse and equally loose-fitting khaki slacks. Later she would admit to Tom that she knew she was young—perhaps only six years older than her students—that the high school boys might find her attractive, and that she had to take appropriate measures."

"You've got to tell us her name, Phil," Amanda insisted.

"I think you know it, Amanda. It's your name." Phil noticed a faint trace of a blush that might have surfaced beneath all that facial hair on the poodle's face.

"Hey, what's going on here?" Sly indignantly bellowed. Does every human have one of our names except me? First there was Pete, Tom's brother, and now there's this Amanda, Tom's supposedly true love. What have we got goin' on here, some weird type of reincarnation thing or something? And by the way, what's happened to Tom's brother and sister? We haven't heard about them for a long time."

"Fair enough questions, Sly, although our mission is to concentrate on Tom. His younger brother had graduated with an engineering degree and found a job in Seattle. His younger sister Grace had completed two years of engineering school and over the summer would become Tom's confidant in his affairs of the heart. But I'm getting ahead of the story."

"So Tom and Amanda will become lovers?" the poodle had surmised. "Go on, Phil."

"During the first week of summer school, before every class, Tom and Amanda would talk briefly out in the hall. Their conversation centered on their students and their absentee supervising teachers, just small talk really. But on Friday after class, without thinking, Tom asked Amanda if she'd like to join him for a late lunch /early dinner.

"She broke into a smile and then in a voice of feigned hurt replied, 'Sure, that might make up for not recognizing me.'

"'What do you mean?' a flustered Tom asked.

"'Last Fall, I saw you every day after soccer practice when I picked up my younger brother.'

"'Oh, I'm sorry. I was, you know, busy, and all. If I would have seen you, I wouldn't have forgotten you.' Now Tom felt like a high school sophomore himself, awkward and embarrassed by his first experience with romance."

"Well, I think it's kinda cute the way Tom is acting. It's as f he's been thrown back in time and given a second chance to re-establish emotional ties, something he hasn't done in years." Amanda observed. Pete either nodded in agreement or was dozing off again. Sly lowered his head and opened his mouth dismissively as if yawning.

But Phil appreciated Amanda's insight. "Good point. This is all part of Tom's re-education. Tom and Amanda (the human Amanda, that is) paused a moment and just looked at each other.

"Then the woman resumed the conversation, teasing him. 'Well, Tom, I know all about you. Last Fall I got a day -to -day summary of your character from my usually unreliable source—my younger brother. He claimed that you were just another old guy, probably in his forties or fifties, trying to relive his lost youth. After the first game in which he saw little action, he also complained that you obviously were blind to true talent and didn't know a thing about the game. He did admit, though, that you weren't in bad physical shape for an old guy in his forties or fifties. But he was a sophomore in high school, you know, a wise fool. I found all of his comments fairly amusing, especially since you won that game, 4-0, and my brother played over a half and in that contest registered nothing in the playbook other than a yellow card for tripping some kid on the other team. He was really irate after you benched him after that yellow card. So, I know all about you, Mr. Tom Albright.'"

"'I know a little about you, Ms. Amanda. And all of my information comes from the same source. Last Fall, you were a senior in college. All the guys on the team thought you were really hot and wanted you to give them a ride home, too. You were, and I presume still are, something of an egghead because you enjoy reading and want to be a teacher. Your brother said that his sister was really weird because she wanted to teach kids like us. You played soccer on a collegiate intramural team and ran 5K races. Most importantly, though, he boasted that your chauffeur duties would soon end, as he would get his driver's license this summer. Did he get his license?'"

"'He did but only after failing the drivers test the first time around.'"

"'Why did he fail the first time? For going too fast?'"

"'No, the resurrected Mario Andretti failed because he went too slow, impeding traffic as the examiner noted. He still drives like an old man, maybe even slower than you do.'"

"'The couple enjoyed a late lunch / early supper at Joey's, a family restaurant in an old Italian neighborhood where you can't walk two blocks without coming across one restaurant after another and all featuring the best pasta in town and plenty of beer and wine to wash down that pasta. They enjoyed some Pasta Primavera and a glass of wine as well as freshly baked Italian bread. They ate outside on a patio, where a light, cool breeze bathed them in comforting caresses.'"

"Wait a minute, Phil. I know what's coming next. Tom is gonna fall in love at first sight. You know, what comes around, goes around. The guy is a sucker for romance, and don't know where the real action is. If that wouldda been me, I wouldda taken her and—"

"Don't say it, Sly. We all know what you would have done or, more likely, tried to do. You're right, though, about one thing. Tom needs to pace his emotions more carefully. He's repressed them for so long that, once unleashed, they run wild and he does crazy things like falling in love at first sight. He needs to go slowly and let Fate work things out."

"You're right, Amanda," Phil remarked. "And Tom gets some help in that arena from a most unlikely source." Phil looked straight at Sly, who uncharacteristically realized that it was time for him to fold and keep his mouth tightly sealed. "Over that long summer, Tom and Amanda went out almost every afternoon. Often they just walked in the park, rehashed the day's triumphs and failures, and all the seemingly banal details that make up the day. They both agreed that they'd limit their restaurant visits to once a week and even then they'd take advantage of the early bird specials to save money. They joked that they were already like an old married couple in that regard. When Tom got home, he sought advice from a most unlikely source, though. He talked to his much younger sister, who would enter her sophomore year in college in the next school year."

"Yeah, when I was little and riding on my mother's back, I talked things over with one of my sisters, too. But I was little then and don't remember much. I think we just complained about the bouncing ride we got. Then momma opossum said that she was preparing us for the much harsher bumps and bruises we would get in our short life spans.

But I remember that I liked talking to her a lot." Pete had been unusually talkative but immediately reverted to his more customary closed-mouth approach.

Phil measured out a faint race of a smile at Pete's revelation before resuming his narrative. "Tom began what came to be nightly conversations with his sister Grace in an offhand way. He came home around ten one night and had a few pieces of pizza left over from a night with Amanda. The couple had gone to a free concert in the park and brought a pizza with them. At first Grace was astonished by two factors completely foreign to her. First, Tom hadn't finished the rest of the pizza himself. That in itself amazed her. 'Tom, what's wrong? I never knew you to not finish off a pizza. Are you sick?" Tom responded that he was feeling fine, that he just wasn't hungry. Then Grace knew what accounted for the change in her brother's appetite. 'Tom, are you falling in love again? I thought you had given up on that.' As soon as Grace let those words slip from her mouth, she immediately recanted. 'I'm sorry, Tom. I didn't want to hurt your feelings. Well, tell me about Amanda. I know that you and she are student teaching at the same school, I know that you two spend almost every waking hour together, I know that you coached her younger brother, and I know that you have completely fallen in love with her. You can't deny any of that, can you?' Tom replied that he couldn't. Then, looking down into his folded hands, admitted that he just feared making the same mistake all over again. Grace stood up and placed her hand on his shoulder. 'Look, Tom, I don't have to tell you to go slow. You don't have the money to move fast. You'll be moving out soon, on your own again. Take your time, save your money, and more importantly check your first impulses. See what time and Fate have I store for you. What will be will be.'

"Tom thanked his sister and, turning away from her so she couldn't see him blush, admitted that the tables were turned. 'As the older brother, I should be the one giving advice, not seeking it out. Thanks, Grace, you're right and echo my own thoughts. I just don't want to risk losing her.'

"'Well, Tom, with the way you're feeling now, it would be more her loss than yours if she let you slip away. I've got a feeling that she won't. I haven't met her yet, but I've got a feeling that the two of you are just so much alike that nothing will keep you apart. For right now, just enjoy the moment.' After that conversation, Tom sat down with his sister Grace to tell her all about how Amanda and he had shared the day together. Grace herself had decided to take a break from any romantic entanglements as she focused on her engineering / pre-med studies. She was taking organic chemistry and yet another physics course over the summer, so she enjoyed these little chats with her brother as a break from the rigor of her studies. Tom enjoyed these private moments with his sister. He regretted only that he had waited so many years to have them.

"By August, before Grace returned to school full-time, Tom put forth to Grace the most difficult question he had ever posed to his much younger sister: How would he introduce Amanda to their parents. 'So you two must be getting serious?' Grace responded when Tom sought some advice from her. When he had introduced Lexie to his parents, he had cavalierly dismissed any misgivings. And had just as equally dismissed their concerns about her. He feared that they wouldn't approve of Amanda for reasons that he might have been blind to. He also feared that their reasons were right and that he might have to break off the relationship he had and the person he had grown to love. Grace thought the matter over when Tom put the question to her. She stood up, walked a few paces over to the kitchen, got herself an iced tea, and calmly sat down. 'Tom, you're missing one important step. Before I give you any advice on how to introduce Amanda to our parents, you've got to introduce her to me.'

"Now Tom stood momentarily paralyzed by the simple logic of Grace's response. 'Of course, I need to introduce the two of them,' he realized."

"Oh, so now he gets it," Sly broke out. "The guy who thought he was so smart, now realizes that he ain't. Well, it's about time. That's all I got to say."

"Thank goodness, Sly at least realizes that," both Amanda and Pete thought. Phil was reserving judgment on the matter to see if Sly would keep his word. Phil stroked his chin and reacted calmly. "It seems that humility is always in short supply among both humans and the rest of the animal kingdom. Let's see what happens."

"Tom asked Grace if she could join them the next evening for the concert in the park. 'It's an informal affair with lots of breaks in between the songs, so there's plenty of time to talk.'"

"Grace stated that it just so happened that she was free tomorrow evening and would be happy to join them. 'But, Tom, you'll have to drive me so we can talk alone in the car when you drop Amanda off.'"

"'Oh, I won't be dropping Amanda off. After the concert, which ends by ten, she's got to pick up her younger brother from a back-to-school party. His parents won't let him drive at night for another month, so she's counting down the days when she no longer has to act as his chauffeur.'"

"'Well, that works out great, Tom. That way we'll have plenty of time to talk in a place where you can't just walk away. Nothing beats the closed confines of a car for some family talks. You know how Mom and Dad would do it. When they were particularly upset or even when they just wanted to get our undivided attention, they'd take us for a drive. Mom told me she'd do the same thing when I was just a baby. She'd take baby-me for a ride just to get me to go asleep. Then, when we all turned teenager on her, she'd take us for a ride just to get our attention.'"

"The concert worked out as the perfect venue not so much for the music but for the chance for Grace to meet Amanda. 'So, this is Tom's way of getting his sister to interrogate me. Well, fair enough. My younger brother has already filled me with information and misinformation about his old soccer coach, so Grace nice to meet you. Let's send Tom on some errand like getting us some popcorn and a drink, so we can get to know each other.' Tom dutifully left, so the two of his favorite women could chat. The line for popcorn was long and the volunteers working the popcorn booth were both inexperienced, so the two women had ample time to talk. Tom never did learn what the two of them talked about. But, when he finally made his way back to them, they were laughing –probably at him. 'I guess I deserve it. Now it's two against one and I have no hope.'

"'Tom, while you're at it, go get us a hot dog. Neither one of us had any supper and we decided to skip our diet plan for one evening and just do the junk food thing.' Tom knew that this was not the time to contradict his sister. Those times lay in the past and the future, so once again he trudged off to the hot dog stand, realizing that he didn't have to rush. He also figured out that in this instance he was almost superfluous. 'Maybe it's a good thing to know when to fold 'em as the song goes.' When he returned with the hot dogs, Grace and Amanda both said in unison, That salty popcorn made us thirsty. Go get us another soda.' Once again, Tom soldiered on, joking that this 'free' concert was costing him far more than he had anticipated. When he got back, the three settled down and listened to the closing song, *Stand By Me*.' Before Grace and Amanda left, they hugged and Amanda gave Tom a most chaste kiss.

"'She's a keeper, Tom. Mom and Dad will love her. You two are so much alike that sometimes I forgot who I was talking to. I think the two you should wait a while—not too long. Go ahead and ask her over for dinner before you move out on your own. I think you should propose at Christmas time if all goes as well as it has been going and maybe get married the following Christmas time. That way the two of you should be able to save up enough money.'"

"'So, the two of you got this all figured out in between bites of popcorn and a few songs?" Tom shook his head in bewilderment and awe."

"'Yeah, pretty much, Tom. Oh, and by the way, I'll be the maid of honor and you better get to know our brother Pete better because he'll be the best man.'"

"'Any other things I ought to know, Grace?'"

"'No, you couldn't expect us to settle everything so quickly, could you? Oh, and by the way, you have one important thing to get working on.'"

"'What's that, Grace? The two of you seem to have everything all planned out.'"

"'The two of us can't do this. It's all up to you.'"

"'What's that?'"

"'You need to get to work on an annulment from your first marriage' Grace replied, her tone shifting to a far more serious note."

"'Yeah, I guess I should,' Tom replied glumly. 'That's something I should have done a long time ago. I just don't know where to start.'" Tom turned his head to the side, so Grace wouldn't see the blush of shame and guilt spreading over his face. But he shouldn't have bothered. His feelings were far too obvious."

"'Tom, what did you do when you needed to talk to someone about Amanda? You turned to me for advice, so who should you turn to now? Who's the one expert you can really trust, someone you respect. You know it's really flattering when you ask someone for help. It means you regard them as an expert. More importantly, it means you respect them. Don't be so shy about seeking help when you need it. Besides, you'll have to return the favor and help me out when the time comes.'"

"Is that time coming soon?' Tom inquired, not sure what answer would be the best."

"'No, not soon, maybe in a few years. I might have to get as old as you are before I figure out that we all need each other at times. We can't go it alone all the time. So, who will you turn to for help on the annulment? Who do you respect the most?'"

"'Father Brennan, the one who gave up his job as president to return to the classroom. He said it was a promotion because now he was back to doing the real mission of the school. And I hear that he knows Canon law backwards and forward.'"

"'There you have it. See, Tom, I've helped you out again, so you owe me big time.'"

"'Yes, I do."

With that, Carrie screeched, "Time's up. See you all next week." Then she took flight.

STAGE ELEVEN

RAISING A NEW GENERATION

T HE NEXT WEEK OPENED A little less contentiously than it usually did. By now Sly had accepted his fate or, perhaps, he realized that the narrative would have to end. It wasn't over, he knew that, but he could see an end point. Sly reasoned that Amanda and Tom wouldn't live happily-ever-after. He knew that no one did in that first life and maybe even in the afterlife.

Phil wasn't quite sure how to regard Sly's newfound docility. Phil couldn't restrain those thoughts in his mind about Sly lying low so he could work out the details of some sinister plot. So, Phil maintained at least one eye on Sly as he resumed the narrative. "Grace had assumed the role of wedding planner. For the most part, she followed her original design. She would have plenty of time to work on the particulars. Tom did propose on Christmas just as Grace had outlined. And the wedding itself was on for the following Christmas. 'That way, the ever practical Grace reasoned, 'the church will be already decorated with flowers, especially poinsettias, so we save money on flowers.' Grace's habit of saying we, as in the expression 'we can save money' indicated that she had internalized Tom's and Amanda's nuptials and was vicariously experiencing her own ceremony. Either that or she was viewing it as a dress rehearsal for her own. Grace determined that Amanda would have four bridesmaids, with herself as maid of honor. When she broached that topic to Amanda, she did so tentatively, only hinting at her own role. She anticipated an objection. But Amanda asked Grace to have the honor of being the Maid of Honor since she had been instrumental in bringing her and Tom together. She had another motive, she confessed. Amanda didn't have a sister, only one younger brother who would serve as one of the groomsmen. She had two very close girlfriends and one cousin who was also close. If Grace served as Maid of Honor, then Amanda wouldn't have to worry about choosing one friend over the other and thereby hurt one friend's feelings. Her cousin was close but not that close. So, that matter was settled quickly between Grace and Amanda. Then remained the question of what to wear. Amanda wanted the bridesmaids to wear red dresses—"

"Wake me when this is over," yawned Sly. "I just want to hear about the honeymoon."

"Yeah, me, too," added Pete. "What's Tom doing all this time?"

Phil's eyes darted over to Carrie and Amanda for any sign of hostility. The two just slightly turned their heads away as if to say, "What else could you expect from those two bozos?" So Phil addressed their question.

"Tom had to address the matter of an annulment. He did seek out Father Brennan at least in an indirect way. He asked him to play tennis, not because Tom was an accomplished player. He wasn't. But he knew that Father Pat Brennan was and he also knew that the fifty year old priest would enjoy trouncing a much younger opponent. Knowing he would lose, Tom also added that the loser would have to buy lunch for the winner. Over lunch, he could introduce the topic of annulment. Father Brennan eagerly agreed. They would play at eleven o'clock on a crisp October morning, just after Tom had concluded soccer practice. The tennis courts lay only a short quarter mile walk from the soccer fields, so all was in order. Tom surprised himself by winning the first game. At first, Tom feared that his plan was unraveling, but he would have nothing to fear. He lost the first set and after that defeat his fate was sealed. Father Brennan liked nothing better than to beat a man half his age and a coach to boot. Tom would have to face the jeers of his comrades for a week or so before everyone would forget about his humbling defeat. Only Tom knew that the defeat would turn out to be a victory. Only after the two had driven over to O'Connell's pub and ordered beers and hamburgers, did Tom ask about the specifics of filing for an annulment. Father Brennan listened attentively as he was well versed in these matters and Tom was not the first one to seek him out for advice. 'You say you don't know where your first wife currently lives. You also say that no one could serve the divorce papers because no one could locate her. How long ago was that?' Tom said three years ago, his head tilted down in shame even after three years. 'Has the divorce been finalized?' Tom responded that after a year and a day it was. 'Well, you need to file the paperwork for the annulment and to pay the filing fee as soon as possible. When do you plan on getting married?' Tom said the wedding was tentatively set for fourteen months away, one year after the next Christmas. 'So, you're saving money on flowers for the church, eh.' Tom felt taken aback. Then Father Pat smiled, and said, 'Well, on your salary you've got to save every penny you can. I wish we could pay the lay teachers more. Look, Tom, I'll do every thing I can to get this pushed through. Before you submit your written responses, let me edit your responses. It all appears as legalistic mumbo-jumbo and sometimes the whole process doesn't seem fair. It's a way to preserve what should be but often isn't a union for life. It's just that people, especially when they're young, make mistakes. So the annulment process recognizes two realities: the ideal of marriage as a union for life and the reality that some people don't fully understand what they're getting into when they marry. It's not like going steady or anything. Don't rush your responses. Think them through carefully before you respond. But it's important to get this paper work filed as soon as possible because the process grinds its way slowly. So, I expect your draft in two weeks. In the meantime, I'll check out my contacts at the tribunal office. Get to work on this tomorrow.'

"Tom didn't get to work on the annulment papers the next day. He started that afternoon and worked through the night until he had completed a rough draft the next morning. When he reviewed his draft that Sunday afternoon, Tom was struck with two realities: 1) he had made so many typos that he had lost count of them; 2) he wished he had answered these questions and prompts thoroughly before he had married the first time. 'But I was young and dumb, unsure of who I was and unsure of what I expected from a lifelong union. I guess Lexie was, too. I wish her no ill will and I hope she found whatever it was she was seeking. Right now, I guess I'm restarting adulthood. Whatever happens, I don't want to harm Amanda in any way. I've been such a fool. As they say, I've been my own worst enemy.'

"Well, Tom revised his drafts four times before he presented a draft to Father Brennan for editing. Then he revised two more times after consultation with the priest / editor. 'You'll still have to try to contact you former wife even though doing so doesn't seem feasible. In any event, you'll have to present evidence of a sincere effort to get in touch with her, so she has an opportunity to respond. If you can't reach her and, apparently, you won't be able to, at least you can show that not even the process servers could find her. I'll explain all of this to the tribunal. In any event don't expect a decision for at least six months. That would mean by next April, you should know. That will give you ample time to prepare for the December wedding.' Tom wasn't sure, but he wondered just how much influence Father Pat exerted at the tribunal: Was he telling him that he already knew that the decision would be rendered next April? In any event, Tom was grateful."

"I know that six months seems like a long time," Amanda the canine, observed, "but, if you consider that marriage should be a lifelong commitment, I guess it isn't all that long. I mean, humans now have a life expectancy that puts them into their late seventies before they pass on."

Sly interjected the following remark, striking a most professorial pose, standing upright as if behind a podium and looking down at his colleagues. "What strikes me is the utter fixation upon laws that humans manifest. They have municipal laws, governing matters like small business licenses; they have state laws pertaining to the sale and distribution of alcohol and marijuana; they have federal laws for interstate commerce; and now we learn that at least some humans also have canon laws regarding some religious matters." Tiring of his act, Sly once again went down on all fours and started grousing. "Yeah, enough of this stuff. You know if humans have a gripe with each other why don't they just settle it, you know, tooth to tooth, claw to claw, mano e mano?"

"Sly, if every dispute were settled that way, only the strong would win? Phil replied. "I guess that would be good for me but not for most."

"Yeah, but the way it works now is that humans still duke it out but it takes high-priced lawyers, high-priced PR firms, high priced bribes, and the like. And for humans the real strength lies in money. So, maybe I was wrong. The humans do duke it out only not hand to hand but bank account to bank account. As for me, I prefer the mano e mano approach."

"Well, Sly," I guess you've got a point. It took a lot of money to catch me and then to keep me locked up all those years, but at least I learned one virtue."

"Yeah, what's that, Phil?"

"Patience."

"Maybe that's why they put you in charge of the four of us. That and the fact that you're as big as a mountain, well, at least as big as a small hill. But I hear that sometimes you'd lose your temper and splash the humans and get them good and wet."

"All right, Sly, now it's time to return to our story." Phil leafed through the volume until he picked up the story two years later, an editorial decision he explained to his audience of four. "I'm jumping ahead two years to the next most significant milestone in Tom's life and development—the birth of his children. I'll just say that he got the annulment although a little later than he had hoped, that the wedding and reception went off without too many glitches, and that the couple found an inexpensive apartment close to the schools where both taught so they needed only one car. They were saving money for a down payment on a house. Everything else went on routinely. In the second April of their marriage, Amanda started with morning sickness. They weren't trying to have a baby. They just were. At first Tom was worried that they wouldn't be able to pay their bills, but the two worked out a plan so that they could. Grace held a baby shower for her sister-in-law in October, for the baby was due in December. That's the background. How are we doing on time, Carrie?"

"Just about half way done."

"Hey, does that mean we get a half-time break, get to grab a few brewskies and brats?" Sly asked as he poked Pete awake.

"Oh, Sly, we meet for only half an hour once a week. What's the problem?" Amanda interjected.

"Well, I thought we just needed to liven things up a little bit. I mean all that dry exposition leaves the throat parched and begging for some liquid refreshment."

Phil just glared at Sly and quietly reflected on his own false hopes. "And I thought that maybe, just maybe, Sly was changing. Maybe he has but not much." Phil waited until all at least looked attentive. Amanda's pregnancy proceeded well but not as planned. On Amanda's first ultrasound, the obstetrician re-entered the room where Tom and Amanda waited anxiously.

'She seems to be taking an awfully long time,' Tom commented as he stood up and gazed out the window at the street scene below. Crowds of people, rich and poor, young and old, bustled along the sidewalk. 'I hope there's not a problem.' Amanda, too, felt uneasy about the delay but didn't say anything. She was too busy praying silently that all would be all right. The physician knocked on the door, opened it, and then casually strolled in asking one innocent sounding question that startled the couple. 'Do twins run in either one of your families?' They turned towards each other with blank faces and mouths slightly agape. Tom was too stunned to respond. Finally Amanda asked, 'Does this mean we're having twins?' The OB nodded her head and joked that she was running a two for one special this week. Tom worried al the more about finances He hadn't anticipated this event. The babies were due at the end of December, with a due date of December thirtieth.

"But the twins wanted to surprise their parents with a Christmas present. At three am on Christmas morning, Amanda started going into labor. Since the temperature had dropped below zero for a week, Tom had been putting the car to bed every night with a trouble-light placed close to the car's battery. He even covered the hood of the car with blankets. He rushed back and forth between Amanda and the car, checking on both nervously. Despite her pains, Amanda tried to comfort her husband's frenetic activity. Finally, she announced, 'It's time to go,' so off Tom went to start up the car, praying that the engine would turn over. At first, the engine faltered like a person groaning to be left alone. On the second try, though, it fired up, and off the couple raced to the hospital."

"You know the problem with humans is that they're way too dramatic," Sly pronounced pontifically.

"Yeah, my mom had six babies and that was nothing for her, at least so I heard," Pete the opossum added.

"Well, the big difference for Tom was that the birth of his daughters made him focus on the miracle of life, on the profound mystery of procreation. When he saw his babies and later held them, he forgot for a moment all the minutiae of life and making a living. 'I am sharing the role of making a living although not in the ordinary meaning of the expression. Sex meant not only a pleasurable moment and an emotional and physical bond with his wife, but a moment of pro-creation. He knew he'd need help in this role. He didn't feel up to the task. He felt overjoyed at the birth as he cradled first one and then the other of his twin daughters. He felt closer than ever to Amanda, who had remained calm throughout the birth. He also felt humbled and utterly inadequate at the task of raising a new generation.

"Now this is where Tom's younger brother, the engineer comes in, not that his engineering degree and job had anything to do with raising children. Pete had come home for the Christmas holidays, still a bachelor, but full of advice for his older brother, most of which was humorous. 'Do you remember, Tom, trying to pass off blame on me for all of your stupid stunts? Like the time when you broke Mom's favorite vase on a cold winter's night just like this one. You were dribbling the soccer in the small confines of the family room when you decided to pass the ball to me. Only you blasted the ball a yard away from me and demolished the vase. Then you claimed that I had done the deed. But Mom didn't buy your story. I'll bet that the twins will run you ragged. You'll never know which one of them did what. Brother, you're about to experience a lifelong exercise in humility.'" When Amanda brought the twins home, Pete joked that his older brother always was an overachiever. 'Most people are content with bringing home one baby at a time, but not my brother Tom. He's got to be twice as good as anyone else, or at least try to be.'

"Tom appreciated his brother's humorous take on the situation. It made him forget for a moment the overwhelming financial needs. 'It was bad enough paying for two car seats, 'Tom moaned. And then there were the sleepless nights. Since he and Amanda had two babies to care for, there was no way he could shirk his role. He'd rock one twin while Amanda nursed the other. Then the two would switch babies. Tom quickly learned to catnap whenever he could."

"Hey, I could have taught him a thing or two about sleeping whenever you can. I know all about it," Pete the opossum bragged, puffing out his chest like a proud father himself.

Phil, Amanda, and Sly held back a laugh and let the comment pass. Carrie was too busy watching her watch to notice.

After that brief pause, Phil determined that he needed to get on with the story. "When Tom wasn't changing diapers or wiping up spit-up or worrying about bills, he wondered about the world their twin daughters would grow up in. He regretted not being closer to his brother and sister. Finally, he valued both of them and wished they had grown up closer. 'I don't know. Maybe it was the age difference. Naw, that's just an excuse. I got myself so wound up in my own problems that I spun around like a top.' Then on a grander stage, he saw a grander tragic-comedy being played out. The actors and actresses would change, but the same plot unfolded. 'Perhaps, the twins can change that,' he mused. He found the world changed but not necessarily for the better. 'At least we're not at war,' he thought, 'not a big one anyway.' Still every month as he wrote check after check after check, he felt drowning in a sea of red ink.

"Amanda shared Tom's hopes and misgivings, but the antics of the twins kept them laughing at least a good part of the time. In public, strangers would approach them and ask, 'Are you twins?' In response, Amanda or Tom or both of them would force a faint smile and the girls would be quiet—at first. After a few years of the same old routine, the twins, especially Bridget, the older one—older by five minutes and thirty-nine seconds anyway—would frown and purse her lips in reply to the question they had heard a thousand times. The younger twin, Meghan, was more inclined to pass off each query with stoic resolve. Finally, when they were both ten, Bridget had had enough. When a stranger approached her and asked the same question, Bridget responded: 'No, we're half-sisters, the same mother with different fathers.' She said it in a smart-ass, off hand way that put a momentary blush on Amanda's face. Later she would laugh about the whole experience. But Meghan didn't like her slightly older sister to steal all of the glory. When the next person asked again, 'Are you twins?' Meghan put on her most serious face and replied: 'No, I'm ten years older but have dwarfism.' Of course, the two of them delighted in confounding teachers who couldn't tell them apart. But they conducted their biggest escapade at age sixteen. Although normally Bridget was the more outspoken one and seemed more extroverted and could face almost any obstacle and tackle it, when faced with the driver's test, she froze. On her first two tries, she failed the test for an accumulation of errors: signaling right when she was turning left, going too slow and thereby impeding traffic, parking two feet away from the curb. By contrast, Meghan passed the test on the first attempt. So the two concocted a ruse. By age sixteen, the two sported slightly different hairstyles. But the differences weren't so great that they couldn't be erased by a few simple strokes of the brush and by minute snips of a scissors. So, in exchange for doing her shift at the restaurant where Bridget worked part-time, Meghan adopted her sister's hairstyle and took the driver's test for her twin. Neither Amanda nor Tom knew of the switch until ten years later. Then they could laugh about the whole incident especially because in those ten years Bridget had garnered two speeding tickets while Meghan had a clean record.

"Still, the bills kept raining down on them. Tom taught, coached, and took on part-time jobs. One summer he worked on commission as a one-man advertising agency for downtown restaurants. In the process, he surprised everyone by making far more money than he had ever anticipated. So, all went well until it came time to pay taxes. Not thinking that he'd ever make much, Tom hadn't paid into Social Security; he also hadn't figured in self-employment taxes; nor had he kept detailed records of legitimate business expenses. By April fifteenth, he realized that he had cleared a dollar an hour less than minimum wage for all his work that previous summer."

"Ya know," Sly intoned professorially, "that's the trouble with government. Here you've got a guy who's tryin' to do best for his family, and the government just takes his money away."

Wanting to change the topic, Amanda the poodle asked, "Did they have any other children?"

At this comment, Phil grew somber and exhaled slowly. "No, they didn't. Amanda had two miscarriages. After those experiences, they decided that they wouldn't try to have any more. Tom felt guilty for feeling some relief when Amanda told him of her second miscarriage. He knew how distraught his wife was. The two held each other and cried. But in his own mind, Tom felt a little less burdened. He didn't know how they could have afforded another child. Then he felt ashamed for what he considered his selfishness. Unfortunately, the miscarriages would serve as harbingers of the sickness and death that would come. Tom realized that he was blessed with his family and thanked God for them. But for the moment, Tom had to make more money."

"Time's up," Carrie cawed as she took flight and circled the skies eternally.

STAGE TWELVE

SQUIRMING IN THE HANDS OF BUREAUCRACY

"Tom found a deal he felt he couldn't refuse," Phil began the next session.

"And those are the kinds ya got to be careful of," Sly warned. Amanda and Pete nodded in agreement.

"Well, you know that Tom and his wife Amanda have had a hard time paying their bills," Phil resumed. "When a car repair bill hit, it hit hard and sent Tom scrambling to find yet another part-time job. He worked security at high school football, hockey, wrestling, and baseball games. He delivered telephone books at least when his car was working. He hustled jobs as a waiter especially at big gala affairs like conventions. Anything to make a buck. Finally, when the twins were in eighth grade and about ready to enter high school, Tom was looking ahead to four years from then. He didn't know how much he afford to help with college tuition. When he started researching the cost of tuition, he shared these sobering thoughts with Amanda. 'When we went to college, we could work full-time in the summer and part-time year round and make enough to cover the cost of tuition. But nowadays, one year of tuition is equivalent to a year's pay. There's no way we could cover it.'

Amanda turned her head to the side as if she were taking in new information that took a little time to process. "You know in my former life, my human would sometimes take me on walks in the nearby college campus. We passed scenic little lakes, metallic sculptures, students playing tennis, and brand new building, stadiums, mini-convention centers, huge student centers. You name it, they got it. I overheard my human speak of how he remembered dorms being almost like barracks. He said that now they resembled hotel suites. I don't see where all these luxuries have much to do with learning."

"You've got a point, Amanda. Sometimes humans and even us lose sight of what's important. Tom was running around so much from job to job that he was losing sight of the more important factors: his relationship with Amanda, Bridget, and Meghan, and with the Big Guy." Phil commented as he looked up from the volume he was reading with passages highlighted in advance so he could summarize significant points.

"Phil, when you say the 'Big Guy,' Sly asked suspiciously.

"No, Sly, by then I had long since passed on. I mean the really big guy, the one who sends you know-where when you pass on."

"Ok, Phil, I was just wondering."

Then Pete the opossum broke his silence. "I'll bet that Tom wasn't gettin' much sleep. You get sort of ornery when you don't get enough sleep."

"You're right, Pete. In that respect, Tom didn't differ at all from everyone else. He found himself snapping at his wife and daughters and then hated himself for doing so. He figured that something had to be done.

"And that something happened in late February of Bridget's and Meghan's eighth grade year. He had to attend a meeting of fellow English teachers in order to fulfill his professional development credentials. At first, all he did was grumble about how the sessions were a monumental waste of time and kept him from making money waiting tables at the Pre-Season of Boating, where people with luxury yachts and lots of money to tip with met and feasted. But during his lunch break, where he dined on bologna and cheese sandwich, he started talking with a teacher from one of the rich, suburban school districts. He casually asked bout the pay scale. The response almost caused him to gag on his sandwich. He couldn't restrain himself from bursting out, 'That's twelve grand over what I'm making now.' He also learned that the stipend for coaching was triple what he earned. He filled out an application the next weekend. As an applicant with a doctorate in English who also coached, he figured that he stood a good chance of getting the job. He interviewed and got it. When he did, he had many second thoughts about leaving the school where he had taught and coached for so many years. But he also knew he had to do it not only for himself but also for Amanda and the twins.

"However, he overlooked that fact that sometimes we just trade in one set of problems for another. In his new position, he didn't snap at his family because of money problems. Instead he bored them whenever he unloaded his frustrations. He recalled learning of the Peter Principle from his college days: 'If you perform well on your job in your current position you will likely be promoted to the next level in the hierarchy of the bureaucracy and so on until you reach the point when you reach your level of incompetence.' Tom acknowledged that the Peter Principle did possess some element of truth to it, but he soon found he had to amend it. He formulated his own principle, the Doubting Thomas Principle: you first have to demonstrate that you are utterly incompetent at your job; then you will be promoted so that the bureaucracy doesn't have to trouble itself with firing you (especially true of governmental bureaucracies); then you will continue to advance through the system, being utterly incompetent at each step until you reach the age of retirement and quickly fade from memory."

"Hey, do ya think that Tom came up with this so-called principle for other motives. I mean, maybe he envied his bosses. Maybe he was bitter about not makin' as much money as they did." Sly accentuated his point by shaking his right forepaw up and down.

"Sly may be right. A lot of people and animals envy those higher up the dog sled than they are," Amanda added.

"Yeah, Sly and Amanda here might be on to something.' Pete added.

Carrie just commented, "In the end they're all just dead meat."

Phil smiled in appreciation. He thought to himself, "You know maybe we're making some progress here. They're questioning and showing a little healthy skepticism." Then Phil spoke to the group. "All of you guys raise some good points. Let me provide you with a few examples and then you can decide for yourselves whether or not the Doubting Thomas Principle has any merit to it. Fair enough?"

All four nodded in agreement, even Carrie.

Tom scheduled his first formal administrative observation eight weeks into the first semester. The assistant principal, Dr. Thompson, inconspicuously slid into the room and eased himself into an empty chair in the back of the classroom It was an Advanced Placement class in English Literature. Tom later learned that the assistant principal had taught middle school social studies for three years before securing an administrative position. The class was discussing the final act of *Macbeth,* especially the lines: it [life] is a tale / Told by an idiot, full of sound and fury, / Signifying nothing.' Some students commented that the whole of Macbeth's life consisted of sound and fury, battle frenzy. Others noted that nihilism and despair might be the end product of bargains with the devil or the witches. Others felt that without his wife, Macbeth was nothing. Five students spoke up, a dozen or more were taking notes, two were nodding off, one of the two sitting in the back next to the assistant principal. In the debriefing session following the observation, Tom knocked dutifully twice on the administrator's door before entering. 'Come in,' he heard and he just as dutifully entered. He stood there for a minute or two while the figure at the large cherry wood desk flipped through some papers. Finally the voice at the desk ordered him to sit down, and Tom did.

"Then the voice broke the silence. 'Your class on Faulkner seemed rather daunting, so daunting that the student next to me was completely disengaged. Why didn't you rope him in and make him part of the conversation?'

'Doctor Thompson, we were discussing Shakespeare's *Macbeth*, not Faulkner's novel *The Sound and the Fury.*'

'Whatever! Content doesn't really matter. You didn't answer my question. Why were you ignoring the student next to me? You must remember that it's our duty to teach all children.'

'In eight weeks, he's shown up to class a total of three times. He hasn't read the material and has no idea of what we're talking about. I've called home and left messages. I went to counseling and learned that he had been placed in my class because he had blank spot in his schedule so his counselor just placed him in AP English because there was an opening there. I talked to him after one class when he did show up and he told me to go ahead and give him an *F* because he didn't need the class for graduation.'

'Well, Tom I appreciate your efforts, but none of those excuse you from not listening to his voice. We're concerned about his feelings. You have a duty to him and to your profession.'

Tom swallowed hard. He felt like responding that Dr. Thompson had a sworn duty to follow up on truant students, that he couldn't engage the student who wasn't there often enough to know what the class was doing and furthermore didn't care. Tom wondered why the school had put the student in a class that he didn't want nor need nor seldom attended. But Tom took the job for money and for his family, so he listened in silence.

'So, Tom, for now I'm evaluating you as *Needs Improvement*. You're dismissed.'

"Tom did an about face and left the room fuming. A colleague, a woman who taught in the room next to his, sensed his anger. 'So, you just came back from your first evaluation with Dr. Thompson. Don't worry. He gives everyone he evaluates a *Needs Improvement* on the first go-round. Then he'll mark you *Satisfactory*, and finally *Outstanding*. It's his way of demonstrating that under his tutelage, you've grown as a teacher. It's just one, big, bureaucratic game.' Over the course of the school year, Tom would learn that his colleague had accurately predicted the path of Dr. Thompson's evaluations. Tom's next assessment marked him as *Satisfactory*, and his third and final one shone in the glory of *Exceeds Expectations*. As for Dr. Thompson's tutelage, there wasn't any.

"As far as Tom could tell, by the end of the year he didn't feel any worry over being fired. In fact, he noticed that a number of teachers routinely violated standards of conduct: they didn't attend the supposedly mandatory faculty meetings—a forgivable infraction since nothing much was accomplished at these; they didn't teach the curriculum; they insisted that students submit work promptly but didn't adhere to the same standards themselves as they graded work at a leisurely pace, sometimes never returning the work to students at all. In short, they viewed themselves as having a sinecure, guaranteed pay for little work."

Aw, Phil, aren't you overdoing it a bit? I mean, there are bad apples in every barrel. Just because one assistant principal plays a silly game about evaluations doesn't mean the whole system stinks." Sly earnestly complained, waving his left forepaw in dismissal of the whole episode.

"Yeah, Sly's got a point," Pete added. "My cousin three times removed discredited the whole opossum species by his antics. He used to raid the henhouses and kill as many hens as he could, not just the ones he ate. You would have thought he was a weasel. But that doesn't mean all opossums are bad."

"I have to agree," Amanda insisted.

"And I would agree, too, if that episode formed the only example. But there are more. Here are two of the most egregious ones. Many teachers played the same game as many administrators did."

"How did they do that?" Amanda asked.

"I'll explain," Phil continued. "Just as that Dr. Thompson played the game of evaluating low and then at the end evaluating high in order to make himself look like the ace mentor, so did many teachers. They were supposed to give two assessments, one at the beginning of the year and one at the end to show that the students had made progress, you know actually learned something. Well, here's how they played the game and stacked the deck. On the first round of the assessments, they repeatedly told the students that the tests wouldn't count for their grade in the class, that they could just take their time and answer only the questions that they were absolutely sure of. The teachers also designed the tests to be unusually difficult. It wasn't hard to do."

"Yeah, I get it," Sly grinned. "Then at the end of the year, the teachers made the test easy and practically gave the answers away and told their students that he test would count for, I don't know, maybe something like fifty per cent of their grade in the course. They sort of gave the hidden message that, if you don't do well on the test, you'd fail. So, almost every single student showed improvement, sometimes lots of improvement. So, the best teachers would often times be the ones who cheated the most. Yeah, I get it, a pretty good scam."

"There's more," Phil remarked. "In order to make the discipline report look good, some of the faculty faked discipline reports. Fewer suspensions mean you've got a better school, right? Students are so intent on their studies that they don't get into trouble, right? Well, here's how this one goes. One dismal day in February—a lot of days in February are dismal with those low-lying dark clouds—Tom was preparing classes during his conference hour, alone in his classroom. Suddenly, he heard screams of 'Fight, Fight' coming from the hallway, so he rushed out to see if he could help calm things down. Two girls were swinging wildly at each other, sometimes grabbing hair and pulling as hard as they could so the floor was littered with bits of hair and drops of blood. Then one of the girls broke free and grabbed a computer from an adjacent classroom and hurled it full force at her opponent. The girl ducked and the computer crashed to the floor without hitting its intended target. So, Tom threw himself between the two girls with his arms outstretched, hoping to establish a momentary truce that might evolve into a cool down period. It didn't. The girl who threw the computer smacked Tom in the back of the head so hard that his glasses flew ten feet away. By then several other teachers and two administrators had rushed in and calmed the girls down. In the aftermath of the fight, one assistant principal wanted to know what Tom had done to provoke the girls. He responded that he didn't know them and had stepped between them in the hope of quieting them down. 'Well, the girl who hit you said she didn't mean to hit you. She was aiming at the other girl when she hit the back of your head.' Tom thought to himself, 'Yeah, I get it. No blood, no foul.' Then the assistant principal added in an offhand way that Tom didn't need to file an incident report. She would take care of the paper work. Neither girl was suspended. Each had to spend the rest of the day in a different administrative office, and that was it. The broken computer still lay on the floor. 'That's it,' Tom realized. He consoled himself with the fact that his glasses weren't broken. But the number of suspensions that February remained unusually low."

"What a scam!" Sly burst out. "High test scores that show phony improvement, phony suspension rates that show phony order. And all for what?' Sly objected.

"So, the admin can show phony data and keep the tax dollars rolling in," Amanda answered. "I've heard of dog breeders who do the same. All looks nice in the kennels open to potential buyers. It looks as if the dogs have plenty of room to roam and plenty of top-quality food to eat, but behind those kennels lie chains and mounds of feces and abused and starved dogs. Humans can be so adept at painting over filth and gilding over their own sins."

"Yeah, I've seen humans deliberately aiming their cars to hit us opossums as we cross the road, just for the fun of it and then laugh and say they were doing us a favor," Pete screamed.

"Don't tell us ya got more to tell us," Sly lamented. "I've heard enough."

"Well," Phil shrugged his enormous, muscular shoulders, "you wanted more examples. "Carrie, how are we doing on time?"

"Pretty good. You've got time for another example, maybe two." With that comment, Sly realized his fate was sealed and resigned himself to patient listening. Amanda wondered how things could get worse.

"The next year, Tom's school got a new principal. His former principal moved on the central administrative office where she enjoyed a twenty per cent increase in pay, a reward for the improved test scores and low suspension rates. She would instruct others in how to accomplish both goals. The new principal, a man in his fifties, prided himself on his ability to instill critical thinking skills in his staff and students. He even had a two foot high miniature replica of Rodin's sculpture *The Thinker* on his desk. However, he directed most of his critical thinking to seducing a twenty-eight year old art teacher, whose husband was suffering from thyroid cancer. He offered to mentor her in how to use art to instill critical thinking. He even gave generously of his time to mentor her after school and on weekends and holidays. To make matters worse, he made no effort to conceal the affair. She and he met in local restaurants. He would chase her down in the hallway, screaming her name, 'Renee, Renee.' Well schooled in the sordid details of adulterous affairs by soap operas and grade B movies, the students quickly caught on to the affair, long before many of the teachers ever did. As a senior prank, some of the students parked a VW convertible in a park about a half mile from the school. Then they used blowup figures and used indelible markers to make them resemble the principal and the art teacher. The principal's contract was not renewed; the affair had gone too public. The art teacher was promoted to assistant principal at a different school in the district."

"Ya know, I guess you can do just about anythin' ya want if you've got good PR. If ya don't, then like that principal guy, ya get the boot." Sly shook his head in disgust, so did Pete.

"I just want to know why the art teacher got promoted," Amanda raised and then stamped her left forepaw down to emphasize her own indignation. "Shouldn't both of them have received the same punishment? And what about the teacher's husband? How did things turn out for him?"

"He's in remission and slowly recovering. It looks as if he'll be all right for a long while. As for the principal, I don't know what happened to him in the long run. I suspect that this wasn't his first fling and probably wouldn't be his last as long as he got a job somewhere. My guess is that he was forced to resign in return for a phony letter of recommendation and then moved on. I wonder about his wife. But, I'm stalling, Amanda. I can't answer your question about the outcome for the art teacher. It was certainly the right call to get her out of the building. Students and parents remember scandals like that for a long time. Maybe the powers that be in her school district thought they could whitewash the whole sordid business by claiming that the principal left for a better position, or at least one more suitable to his unique talents and the art teacher won a well-deserved promotion for her good work. All bureaucracies hate scandals and will do anything to slap a happy face on anything."

"Ya know, as one well-acquainted with human trash and the stuff they don't want to go public, I've got to agree with Phil there."

"Oh, I'm also sure that Phil is right, but it makes me sad to think that that's how bureaucracies work. It seems that humans have constructed structures and systems they can't control. That's the stuff for a real horror story. But, Phil, what's the outcome for Tom? He must have known about the whole business." Amanda had turned her head sideways, straining to process all that Phil had described.

"Amanda, at first Tom remained one of the last to know. He had focused all his efforts at work to teaching his students, both the high and the low achievers. He couldn't save everyone and he didn't think he was any type of Messiah. He just wanted to do his job. When he learned of the affair, he shrugged his shoulders as if to say,' That's the way of the world.' In a strange twist, he returned to prayer, the simple faith of childhood, and just tried to do his best as a teacher, husband, father, and citizen. He knew he was no saint, not by a long shot. But he tried."

"Time's up," Carrie cawed out as she took flight and soared through the heavens.

STAGE THIRTEEN

COPING WITH WAR, DISEASE, AND DEATH

THE NEXT WEEK, PHIL LUMBERED into the Convocation Area slowly as if burdened by a heavy load. "Well, my friends, this week's discussion may sadden us all." He paused for emphasis and also to hold back from saying what thoughts lay in the back of his mind. He almost added, "may sadden us all—except for one of us" but he thought better and left the afterthought out. With his enormous head downcast, he appeared sad and gloomy.

"Phil, are you all right? Amanda asked earnestly.

"I'm fine. It's just that Tom had to deal with war, disease, and death—not very pleasant topics. He couldn't withdraw into a private world and live in a cloister. He had to rethink his whole approach.

"On the morning of September eleventh, 2001 Tom was working one-on-one with students three or more years behind in their reading skills. He also knew that all but three of the seventeen were equally behind in their math skills. Most came from poor families; only three, all with Special School district Individual Educational Programs, had middle class backgrounds. The public school, which advertised itself as serving all students, dished out a watered down version of a college prep curriculum to all students. Tom felt that many of the students would benefit more from some form of technical training, but as an individual teacher, he couldn't do much other than to help them as much as he could. After all, prestige and the accompanying tax dollars all flowed from good publicity and that publicity sprung from such data as college matriculation rates. Tom observed that there was no follow up data on college graduation rates. All

131

he could do, he felt, was to do the best job he could under the conditions dictated from on high. Somehow, those in the bureaucracy, especially many administrators though certainly not all, didn't view themselves as ever returning to teaching, one of the two main goals of the school—the other one being learning. One could only hope that improved learning would naturally flow from improved teaching—but only the lesser sorts actually taught, so it went. Tom would limit himself to his private sphere and do what he could, relatively immune from outside influences.

Then at 8: 46 am Eastern Time (7:46, Central), Tom's private castle walls collapsed as the walls of the North Wall s of the Twin Towers came crashing down. Roughly fifteen minutes into the first period, the usual routine ended. Shortly afterwards, Tom heard screaming coming from the hallways. He assumed that students were, once again, fighting in the hallways. He rushed out to see some students crying, some sobbing, and others dazed.

"'What's going on?' he asked a fellow teacher who was standing in the hallway.

"'Haven't you heard?' she responded. Tom gave her a blank stare. 'One of the Twin Towers in New York was hit by an airplane in a terrorist attack.'"

"'In the background, Tom heard students, chattering. 'This means war,' one shouted. Some of these students would later call military recruiters, the same recruiters who had been discouraged from doing their work at school by many not-so-very-subtle means. The bell signaled the start of the next class, but many students remained in the hallway, a few hugging each other, a few walking about randomly, and a small number vowing to get revenge. Then an announcement sounded out over the PA system. The anonymous voice urged calm. Gradually students and staff alike recovered somewhat from the initial shock. However, some teachers had wheeled in TV's and whole classes watched the ruin and havoc. The second attack occurring at 8:03 Central time dismissed any assumptions that the first one was only an isolated terrorist event. Too much chaos was streaming through the veins not only of New Yorkers but also even of adolescents in the far off Midwest. Then, when news that the Pentagon had also suffered an attack, all feared that war against some unknown enemy would follow. Some of the senior boys who had turned eighteen and had just registered for the draft looked at each other glumly. Tom overheard one boy saying: 'I thought this whole Selective Service thing was a joke. I mean, no one's been drafted in what, like thirty years. I guess the joke is over.'

"But war wasn't immediately forthcoming. No one was sure of who the enemy was nor where the enemy harbored itself. Those issues would be addressed later. Still, the death of 2,977 people, mainly Americans but also citizens of the UK, the Dominican Republic, and even of India, and ninety other countries died. And many more would die later, victims of cancer from the smoldering ruin. For the survivors and spectators of the attack, the emotional toll defied measurement. School ended early that day. Many students went home and watched in horrid fascination the collapse of the twin towers over and over again. Their world and their assumptions of the world were collapsing.

"Tom's assumptions, too, struck him as sophomorically naïve. He recalled the philosophy teacher who claimed that the threat of nuclear war had rendered war itself obsolete, an anachronism in the modern world. During the pointless futility of Viet Nam, his argument seduced many. The Age of Aquarius was coming, some argued. War, religion, ethnic and cultural conflicts would exist only in the history books, so some said. Now, Tom and many others like him were shifting to new beliefs that they wished they could dismiss as bedtime nightmares. But the nightmares had become real. For a moment, Tom felt relieved that his two children were girls, safe for the moment from the draft. Then, he felt guilty and both felt both sorrow and pride at those who had served and died and for those who suffered lifelong injuries. He thought of his father, reeling round and round in the horrid dance of an epileptic fit, the result of war injuries."

"When humans wage war, it seems that no one wins. Even the victors suffer," Amanda remarked.

"Yeah, right, but there wasn't any world war or anything," Sly observed.

"I don't like this part of the story," Pete complained.

Carrie only grinned.

"When I shuffled in, you all could tell that I didn't like this part of the story either. But did have one good outcome." Phil struck a meditative pose, standing solemnly like the statue of a saint, eyes fixed straight ahead, one arm at his side, the other holding the book of Tom's life. The only feature lacking was a halo circling above his head.

"What's the good outcome, Phil?" Amanda asked Amanda asked as she gazed directly at Phil's eyes.

"Yeah, I don't see what good could have come of this," Sly objected. I mean I know somethin' about what the humans call 'current events.' Haven't there been just war after war since that 9-11 attack. I mean I heard about two different wars in Iraq and another one that's still goin' on in Afghanistan. And terrorist attacks are goin' on all over the place."

"You're right, Sly. Tom had so engrossed himself in his own little world that he had just sort of glossed over the holocaust that had taken place in Rwanda, not far from where my own ancestors had lived. Then, there was the ethnic cleansing in Bosnia. Then two years later the genocide in Sudan, one that's still simmering every now and then. It seems that humans can't stop killing each other. Closer to home, there's the narco wars in Mexico and the gang wars in American cities. Humans have created their own hell."

"You know, I've heard that some humans even train dogs and roosters to fight to the death, just the way the humans do—well, not with guns or anything, but they still school the poor animals in cruelty." Amanda shook her head in disgust.

"Well, ya know, humans aren't alone in their cruelty. I've heard of a fox or a weasel takin' their good ole time killin' some poor opossum that fell into their grip." Pete almost shuddered just thinking about it. I mean, some of the humans who try to run us over when we're just crossin' the street are bad, but so are other predators. It's just a cycle that keeps goin' on and on. But what does it all mean?" Exhausted by the longest speech of his existence, Pete lay down, not asleep but worn out.

"This is where the good effect—well, good at least for Tom—comes in. Pete's question is a good one. Just what does it all mean? Tom reflected for a long time. He wanted a better world for his daughters, Bridget and Meghan. He wanted to live out his years in peace with Amanda his wife, who had been so loving and patient with him. But he couldn't create this ideal world by himself, nor even with the added strength of Amanda. The world wasn't perfect and neither was he. So, imperfect societies and imperfect individuals create imperfect worlds. In accepting his limitations and those of society, Tom was beginning to learn humility. In learning humility, he turned back to prayer."

"Maybe there wouldn't be so much conflict if everyone practiced some humility," Amanda observed.

"Unfortunately, Tom would experience even more lessons in humility. His efforts to establish his own private kingdom of tranquility would suffer severe attacks from forces he couldn't control.

"Two years after the 9-11 attacks, Tom's father died, just five months after he had retired. Tom still recalls his father's retirement party: throngs of people he didn't know, a few relatives and neighbors he did, and more food than he could imagine. An uncle trucked in two kegs of beer to the outdoor party in the park, where children enjoyed some pickup hoc-soc games or fishing in the nearby lake. Adults made sandwiches for themselves and drank beer from red solo cups with their names written in permanent marker. The only sure way Tom could greet people he didn't recognize was to spy their names written on the cups, but that technique had an uneven success rate. Still, people enjoyed the June sunshine and cool breezes and just being together."

"Ya know, that's another thing I don't get about humans. They work almost all of their lives and then retire and try to take it easy. I think I was retired all my life"

Amanda shot Sly the glance of the evil eye, which told him to keep quiet so Phil could finish the narrative. Still, she had to admit at least to herself that Sly had a point. Pete had dozed off and was only half listening, so he didn't care.

"Then," Phil resumed, "Tom learned three weeks after the retirement party that his father was dying and his mother was quickly declining. His parents had hoped to spend at least a little time enjoying their newfound freedom from work. At age sixty-eight, his father had hoped that he and his wife could travel a little around the country and spend more time with their adult children and two grandchildren. Tom remembered his father's saying, 'We'd be grateful for five more years together,' They had five months, most of which they spent assuming the role of nurse for each other. Tom recalled sitting at his father's bedside as his mother lay in the bed beside him, both gasping for air and probably, privately hoping for a quick end to their pain. When Tom heard the death rattle and heard his father's head drop back on the pillow, he knew it was over. He never told anyone, not even his wife Amanda that he felt the presence of some spirit close by, hovering in a dark corner and shrieking what must have been the banshee's wail. Tom tried to erase that sound from his mind, dismissing it as just the invention of his own tortured soul, but twenty years later and for the rest of his life he would still recall that horrid sound. He heard that wail again at his mother's bedside a year later. Tom's mother had lived as a very independent woman, working either part-time when her children were young or full time when they entered school. She had taught them to read and do basic arithmetic even before they entered kindergarten. She also instilled in them the value of living within one's means—plenty of good times but no extravagance. Some of her friends joked that she was so tight that she squeaked. At her death, Tom couldn't believe that he had heard that penetrating wail again."

"Tell us, Phil, did Tom really hear that wail or was his feverish mind just bringing to Tom's ear the memory of some childhood fairytale?" Amanda asked, sitting attentively at the feet of Phil.

"Amanda, like a lot of other things, I don't have authorization to know one way or another. Sometimes it's hard to unravel fact from fiction because the mind does strange things to reality. It takes a sensory impression—like maybe the wind blowing, and then wraps it in all types of emotions—fears of the unknown, past memories both factual and fictional, and all of other things that we'll never know. The memory of that wail did have one lasting impact on Tom, however. It made him take a closer look at his life. The death of parents makes a person realize that generational death barrier is buried along with the dead parents. Humans have to face the reality of their own deaths, and that's hard for them to do since they've spent most of their lives burying themselves in work and in play and in doing whatever they can to blot out the one reality they can't escape. Tom began assessing his own life, regretting the times he snapped at his wife, disciplined his twin daughters a little too harshly, didn't do too much to help the poor, was too arrogant to ask for forgiveness. He began to look at his life and found it just one, long string of regrets over what could have been but wasn't. Finding himself unequal to the task, he began to pray more earnestly and to try to do his best to help others. In this regard, he looked to his wife for guidance. Her parents still lived—but not for long as it turned out—but she had been far more loving than he had ever been, and Tom knew it."

"Yeah," Sly commented, "Ya don't know what you've got until you lose it." Phil and Amanda both reacted to Sly's remark similarly. The two tried to detect any hint of sarcasm in Sly's voice but couldn't sense any. Maybe the saying was trite, but then again, they both reflected, a lot of trite sayings have a basis in truth. Sometimes that basis is strong and sometimes it's weak. But it's there. In this instance, Sly was sincere. So was Pete when he said that he wished he could restart his former life and do it all over again—only better.

"Unfortunately," Phil continued, "those weren't the only deaths. Amanda's father died of a heart attack three years after Tom's mother had passed. Tom had tried to be as attentive as he could be, but he also realized that grief grew in three very different dimensions: public and social, familial and sensitive, personal and intense. The funeral itself expressed the public grief over a man who had done his duty to his country, himself, and his family not that there weren't any tarnishes. On occasion, he drank too much, failed in his duty especially to his family. But the number of those occasions shrank more and more as he aged. Still, he overcame alcoholism and that in itself is an accomplishment. He had done far more than that, though. Only his wife and children knew how much he cared for them even when he had had one too many. He never abused anyone but himself, and in his later years he tried to make emends for all his earlier failures. His wife and children, especially Amanda, enjoyed talking about and reminiscing about how he had made every family outing to the park a momentous occasion. Once, he rented a boat and piloted them all about, barking out orders like a Captain Ahab. When John, Amanda's younger brother, hauled in a bluegill, he presided over the whale of an adventure. Christmas for him always remained special and he tried his best to make it special for everyone else. Amanda and her brothers reminisced fondly over all of their father's antics and laughed and laughed. But then there was Amanda's very private grief, and often Tom realized that he should respect her privacy and not intrude.

"When, five years later, Amanda's mother slowly passed away with a three and a half year bout with pancreatic cancer. She never complained of her pain and discomfort—except to Amanda. She continued to work up to the time she entered hospice. Tom and Amanda adapted her house to suit her new needs, moving her bed downstairs. They also did her laundry and brought her food and gave he sponge baths. Every day, Amanda, frequented accompanied by either Bridget or Meghan or both, stayed with her several hours. Tom visited and checked in with her every other day. Her only concern was that the grandchildren, Amanda's brother's children, and Amanda's two grown children, the twins, would have a good Christmas. Even though Meghan and Bridget had turned eighteen, she still thought of them as children in a sense. In many other respects, though, she regarded them as adults and heirs to her own taste in fine clothes bought on a limited budget. For her two favorite girls, she bought two outfits in the latest style. When she finally passed, she did so quietly without fanfare. Tom, Amanda, Meghan and Bridget all wept together and then went about the process of arranging for the public grief. Whether Amanda ever heard that piercing shrill cry at the moment of her mother's death, Tom never knew. He had not heard it himself and felt shy of intruding upon her most personal grief."

"That's so sad," Amanda concluded. Even Sly, Pete, and Carrie nodded in agreement.

"Sadder yet was the grief that almost Broke Tom," Phil continued. "As sad as these deaths were, they still at least seemed part of a natural cycle. Those people had lived good lives. They never basked in the limelight or pounded some obstreperous public gavel, but they did their job well, loved their families, and passed on to a better life. What happened next nearly broke Tom and killed Amanda.

"Amanda had had a few scares before. Routine examinations had detected small lumps but they had had been benign. That had occurred twice, once in 2001 and then again in 2004. 2007 would prove otherwise. Tom had accompanied Amanda to the breast cancer center and kept telling himself and Amanda that all would be well, that this was just another incidence of benign tumors, that they had nothing to worry about. This time, though, Tom didn't even convince himself. The physician referred Amanda to a surgeon who would perform the brief procedure. Again, Tom maintained that all would be well, that there was nothing to worry about. Amanda didn't say anything, but her silence convinced Tom that there really was something to worry about. So, he stopped the naïve denials, and the whole family silently and nervously awaited the results. At this time, Tom realized that Amanda's possible breast cancer would also deeply affect the twins, Meghan and Bridget. He had always envisioned the twins as children, running downstairs to open Christmas presents, playing soccer, swinging wildly on the playground in the park. Now Tom had to admit that the twins had grown into young women and that they, too, might face that devastating diagnosis. The weekend following the operation found the whole household pretending that all was normal. It wasn't. The following Monday at ten am, Amanda received a call that the tumor was malignant. She immediately scheduled appointments with an oncologist and a surgeon. It didn't take her long for all weekend she had researched her options and had prepared for what she knew was the inevitable outcome. The consultations confirmed her insight. She would have to have a mastectomy. She scheduled a double mastectomy and then rounds of chemotherapy and radiation. Tom was more visibly upset than Amanda, who busied herself with the particulars of the procedure with all the appearances of almost clinical detachment. But Tom sensed her fear. She was facing pain, disfigurement, and possibly death. Tom felt guilty for momentarily feeling sorry for himself: he just wasn't prepared to be a widower just yet."

"Oftentimes, I've noticed that females and males experience fear in different ways. When one is strong, the other is weak. And then the roles reverse." Amanda commented almost clinically as if she had studied the matter thoroughly, and, in a sense, she had. Living with humans, she had spent years observing them, especially their emotions, which she comprehended fully.

"Ya know," Sly added. "Amanda's right on target." Pete nodded in agreement.

Phil took the reactions of his colleagues as a signal to move on. "Amanda maintained her controlled composure until the morning of the operation. Then she collapsed into tears, flooding her face.

"Tom hugged her gently and wiped away her tears with a kiss. 'It'll be all right,' he reassured her.

"'Tom, I'm so cold, so cold,' Amanda shuddered. Tom looked up in horror. 'Tom, you've pulled the sheet off me. I'm freezing.'

"Tom apologized feebly. Amanda laughed in response. 'Tom, you're cute when you're apologizing. Tell Bridget and Meghan I love them.'

"I will. We'll all be waiting for you. It'll be all right.' Tom wasn't trying to reassure only Amanda but himself and Bridget and Meghan as well.

They were pacing the floor in the waiting room when Tom joined them. The three tried to kill time with small talk. It didn't work as one by one each nervously glanced up at the clock. Then they tried playing cards, rummy, their favorite game. That took their minds off their fears for a while, but soon even that diversion proved ineffective. Tom felt as if his stomach were twitching, jabbed by a thousand little pricks. He looked at Bridget and Meghan. They, too, must have felt that same sensation like a sewing machine sticking them hundreds of times a minute.

"Finally, the operation was over—a success so it seemed. But the pain didn't end with the surgery. Amanda had tubes projecting from both sides of her chest. Even when the tubes had accomplished their mission, the treatment continued. Then rounds of chemo and radiation followed. Tom recalled a trip to the wig shop after Amanda had lost her hair. 'What do you think, Tom?' From long experience, Tom knew how to respond. He replied that she looked gorgeous. 'Well, Tom, you were always a lousy liar. I feel like a like a bad version of Dolly Parton, minus the big boobs.' After that experience, Tom left with Amanda to pick out some colorful headscarves, chemo beanies, they were called. Tom had to admit that the chemo beanies were an improvement over the wigs at least for Amanda. More importantly, he admired the way Amanda had faced the fear, pain, and possibility of imminent death. He wasn't sure he could do the same."

"Yeah, so what did the poor slob do?" Sly asked more in pity than in reproach.

"Well," Phil reflected, he did two things: he prayed and he realized that no one can do it alone." Phil thought for a moment about adding "even you" to his answer to Sly, figuring that little by little Sly was making progress.

Then quickly turning towards Carrie, Phil asked, "How are we doing on time, Carrie?"

"Oh, maybe thirty seconds or so left." Phil guessed that they might have been over the time limit, but, once again, he sensed that even Carrie had softened a bit.

"Next week, my friends, same time, same place."

STAGE FOURTEEN

WRAPPING THINGS UP

S LY ALMOST BOUNDED INTO THE Convocation Area, chortling to himself, "I hear that this is it; the time to put ole Tommy-boy to rest. I can't wait."

Pete looked up his friend with his eyes narrowed in a puzzled expression. "I don't know, Sly, this really hasn't been that bad. I mean, it's like getting a new insight on humans. Not all of them are revving up their car engines, ready to run us down on the road. I'll bet that Tom never intentionally went out of his way to steer his car over us."

"You're on, Pete. How about we place a tenth of a dumpster load of garbage on the bet?"

"I don't know, Sly. That's a helluva lot of garbage."

"Not so sure now, are ya, Pete?"

Pete bristled at Sly's remark. "Look, Sly, I'm no chicken. I'm an opossum. We're on."

"Then it's a deal?" Sly grinned, anticipating an easy win.

"We're on."

"What are you two talking about?" Amanda asked, eyeing each of them suspiciously.

"Oh, nothing much," Sly retorted. "Just a little wager between me and Pete here. Ya might not get it, Amanda. I mean, it's sortta a guy thing."

"Oh, I think I get it completely. One or both of you two are being foolish."

"Now, where would you get that idea?" Sly snickered.

Just then Carrie swooped down, precisely one minute before the

141

scheduled start. Thirty seconds later, Phil steeped in, carrying the volumes of Tom's life close to his chest.

"Hey, Phil," Sly asked, looking up and trying his best to appear earnest. "There's just one thing that's been buggin' me and Pete here. Now in the former life both of our species have been the target of vehicular animalslaughter, right?"

"Unfortunately, yes," Phil intoned solemnly.

"Well, Pete here and I just gotta know. Did that human, the subject of our inquiry, ever directly endanger or kill one of our species by steering his car in our direction and thereby causing great bodily harm or even death?"

"No," Phil scratched the top of his head as if trying to pluck the answer from his brain. "There's nothing in the record of Tom's ever trying to overrun any animal. Once he accidentally hit a squirrel that darted out in front of him and then tried to double back and do a U-turn. There was no way he could have avoided hitting the squirrel. Other than that incident, the record speaks nothing of any road kills, intentional or otherwise."

"Are you sure?" Sly asked in a frenzy, his tail twitching this way and that. "Let me take a look at those volumes."

"Sure, Sly, no problem," Phil responded guessing (correctly as it turned out) why Sly suddenly panicked. Phil slowly and gently placed all the volumes in front of Sly, one after the other in a neat row. Sly looked up at Phil and swallowed hard.

Amanda grinned and said softly, "Sly, why don't you try looking at the index in the back of the last volume."

"Oh, yeah, the index, well, sure. I was just about to check that index-thingie out." Sly gulped hard, and pawed his way through the index. "Let's see here, nothing under raccoon, nothing under opossum, nothing under traffic accidents, nothing under runovers, nothing under traffic accidents, nothing under animalicide. Yeah, I guess that Tom didn't. Of course, there's always the possibility that Tom's historian may have missed something, right, Phil?"

Phil just shot Sly a look that said, "You've got to be kidding me."

"Pay up, Sly, one tenth of a dumpster full, I believe was the wager."

"Yeah, Pete, about that one tenth bit. I was just engagin' in a little of what do ya call it, yeah, hyperbole, that's the word. I didn't really mean one tenth. I was referring to a tenth of a tenth or maybe less."

"Or maybe you're just full of BS," Pete said. "You know, Sly, I never figured you'd make good on the wager. I just enjoy beatin' ya for once."

Sly slunk over to a remote corner of the Convocation area as far from Pete as he could get and yet still listen to the proceedings.

Amanda shook her head and then her whole body and thought to herself, "I knew this is the way it would turn out."

Celebrating his victory, Pete opened up. "So, Phil, are we going to hear the rest of Tom's story, you know, the part about his dying and all?"

"No, Pete, that's not our task. And we don't get to judge him. That task is left to higher authorities than the five of us. We just get to make recommendation on Tom based upon what we've heard and discussed."

"Well, Tom is no saint but he's also no terrible sinner. A lot of the time he dwells too much on his own problems and doesn't think enough of others. But sometimes he can be sweet and loving, too. I guess he's just an average sort of guy." Amanda spoke decisively, leaving no room for doubt, equivocation, or rationalization.

"Ya know, I guess Amanda's right. The guy ain't no saint, and I guess I've run across my share of humans a lot worse than that guy Tom. Anyways, if we ain't judgin' him, then what have we been doin' all these fourteen weeks"

"Yeah, I couldda been sleepin' in all that time," Pete protested.

"You guys need to challenge yourselves a little more," Amanda pointed out. "In these past few weeks, we've gotten to learn about an average human, not all good, not all bad. Maybe he's just a lot like us. We're not exactly perfect, you know."

Pete ruminated a bit over Amanda's comments. "Amanda's right. Sly ain't exactly a model of humility. And, as for me, well, I do indulge in sloth and sometimes I gorge myself sick. These sessions have gotten me off my duff and into the real world, doin' somethin' other than just eatin' and sleepin'."

Sly wasn't convinced but knew he was outnumbered, so he tried a slightly different approach. "Ya know, nobody's answered my question. If we ain't judgin' ole Tom-boy, then what are we doin'?"

"A fair enough question, Sly," Phil responded. "But, if you think over what Amanda said, you'd reach a startling insight. These sessions are not just about Tom. They're about us." Phil stressed his point by stretching his arms out as wide as they could reach and then thrusting them in towards his chest.

Now Sly was more puzzled than ever. "How can this be about us? I mean, ain't we in heaven. You know everything's perfect and we just got the good life, even if it is a second life."

"Who told you this is heaven?" Phil asked, stifling a laugh.

"Well, I don't see no flames, I don't smell no brimstone. I got it pretty good, considering." Sly looked around as if taking in a panoramic scene of beauty. And he was.

"You're a little right and a little wrong, Sly. No, you don't feel the torments of hell. But you also don't feel the ecstasy of heaven."

"For real, Phil? You've got to be kiddin' me. So, if this place ain't heaven and it ain't hell, then it must be—"

"Purgatory. "Phil interrupted. You get a chance to refine yourself, improve upon your outlook on the self and the world before you make the great leap."

"Yeah, yeah, yeah, and just how would you know, Phil? Have you been there? I mean to heaven and all."

Phil nodded. "Sometimes I get to go down here on special assignment. It's good for me, and I hope it's been good for you. I don't judge, and neither should any of us. We don't get the last call. But, Sly, to return to your original question. You know the ending of the 'Hail Mary' prayer— 'pray for us now and at the hour of our death'?"

"Yeah, I've heard it."

"Well, we get to pass on recommendations about how much interceding Mary should do. What do you think?"

"Tom isn't a bad guy, but he probably needs a lot of interceding," Amanda reflected.

"Yeah, Amanda's right," Pete seconded.

Carrie nodded in agreement.

Sly looked around and reluctantly yielded to what was becoming a consensus. Then he paused and asked, "So, what do we get out of this?"

"Sly, let me answer your question with another one. In your first life, did you ever talk with other species? Did you ever get to think and reason and even to disagree and sometimes change your mind?" Phil directed his gaze not just at Sly but also at the whole convocation of five, including himself.

"Come to think of it, no," Sly stressed the *no* by booming his voice into a resounding *no*. Then he paused, rubbing his chin with his right forepaw. "So, you're sortta tellin' us that purgatory can be a sortta school?"

"Yes, Sly, you're right not always, but sometimes."

"Whoa, Phil, are you sayin' that about me or about purgatory?"

Phil grinned, showing an immense expanse of teeth. Then, he responded quietly, "Both."

"Let me get this all straight in my head. We came to this afterlife and were sent to this purgatory place where we get time to think things out and get our heads straight. And, you, Phil, you're some type of heavenly messenger on special assignment to lead us to a better place—that is, if we pass the final examination, right? So, all this time, all fourteen weeks, isn't just about Tom. It's about us and how we react, right?"

"You're right on both counts, Sly. I couldn't have said it better myself."

STAGE FIFTEEN

ACKNOWLEDGEMENTS

NONE OF THIS TALE WOULD have been even fictionally possible were it not for the groundbreaking work of the famed zoo-linguist, Dlorah Yelnoc. In his first life Professor Yelnoc devoted his life to the study of communication among mammalian species, such as the humpback whales and the great apes. Then, when he passed on to purgatory, he and Phil worked on an inter-species language so that all of God's creatures could share in talk and, as a corollary, in reasoning. Only by his and Phil's constant devotion could these convocations take place.

Printed in the United States
by Baker & Taylor Publisher Services